GLOSSARY

Oni—a kind of yókai, ogre, or troll in Japanese folklore.

Shikigami—a kind of spirit summoned to serve a practitioner of onmyódó.

Onmyódó—a traditional Japanese esoteric cosmology, a mixture of natural science and occultism.

Wara ningyo; "straw dolls"—a type of doll made in Japan. They can be used to represent people, or aspects of people, in much the same way as voodoo dolls in the west.

Ofuda—a type of household amulet or talisman, issued by a Shinto shrine.

DEDICATION

For the two little beams of sunshine in my life who make me believe anything is possible. For the friends and family who've supported me during this transition and throughout my life, I couldn't do this without you. For Papa. I'll miss you forever.

NECROMANCER FOR HIRE

NIGHT HUNT

ISA MIKAELSON

Chapter One

Warlocks are temperamental bastards—used to having whatever they want available with a swift spell. They tend to expect everything to happen on their grossly accelerated time frame. Of course, they happen to pay handsomely for their impatience. Which is why I'm out at midnight, with a satchel full of crystals, herbs, and one of my all-purpose spell books. You never know what you might need to do when dealing with business mergers. I flip the collar of my angular black wool peacoat up to block out the wind blowing through the open space, ready to race down my collar and disrupt the warmth I've retained thanks to layers and, a bit of magical assistance.

The night air is turned frigid with the breeze off the

ocean, adding dampness that creates an unrelenting chill that cuts bone-deep. My business in the Underground and the bright pink *final notice* envelopes pulled me from my cozy wingback chair in front of the fireplace. In the late eighteenth century, Seattle burned, and the good people decided to build right over it. The deaths and location of naturally formed portals created a separate plane of existence. A combination of their careless abandonment and improper rebuilding, sealed off any chance of shutting down the gateway.

If the magical community hadn't trickled into the hidden places, manipulating the excess otherworldly energy and policing the gates to control what came out, the town would have seen more tragedy. As the darkness needs the light to have balance, so is the way with magic. Approaching the small, unassuming building in the middle of Cherry Street, I descend the stone stairs navigating to the heavy wooden door.

I grab the round metal knob. A burst of energy travels down my spine as the ward recognizes me as kin. The lock releases. Pushing inward, I cross the veil that separates the world above from the one below and enter the Underground. Tingles travel the length of my body. To anyone nonmagical, this door would lead to a set of refurbished pathways that commemorated history frequented by tourists and guides. For magical wielders like me, it's a completely different world.

Brackish sea air yields to warmth and the rich, moist scent of earth. The curved brick archway overhead contrasts with the dirt path lined with trees on either side. A strip of chocolate brown soil winds through the impossible woods into a bustling city. The smell of cinnamon and sugar make my stomach rumble as I pass the churro shop on the corner.

Slowing, I visually molest the golden pieces of star-shaped bread glistening under carefully aimed and effective lighting. The nearly negative number in my bank account flashes in my head, dissuading me from stopping. Living on Ramen, soup, and tuna got old two weeks ago. There's only so many ways to spice up the college student staple. At twenty-one, I'm over this particular *survival diet*. Work's been slow. Not that the bills cared.

Ignoring my protesting stomach, I move away from the shop window, weaving through the crowded cobbled stone streets toward my final destination. A few nod in recognition while others provide a wide birth. Returning the acknowledgment, I let the shunning slide off the barrier I've erected around my emotions. The approval of others ceased to affect me a long time ago. Simply being Ezra Zaan placed me in a situation that would've broken a lesser person.

As my grandmother would say, *fools were better seen than heard*. Minding your business has merit. It's helped me thrive after relocating to the city. The notorious *Seattle freeze* proved there was nothing new under the sun. In the small, dreary community, forming true friendships took time. My tiny circle of loyal friends took over five years to amass, but they were worth it.

Conjure loomed ahead on the corner. The three-story brick pub housed a speakeasy-style lower level where a number of questionable *business transactions* were forged. Tinted windows kept the atmosphere the same regardless of time of day. Like a Vegas casino, Conjure created an environment where time no longer existed. Though it can't be said that everything that happens here stays here.

Disputes and shadiness often spill over into the world outside. Low lighting illuminated exposed brick and dark wooden floors. The round tables and the bar are packed with people imbibing various drinks. I traverse the crowded main room on the first floor, carefully pacing myself to blend in. Reaching the end of the hallway that houses the bathroom, I knock on the wall. A hidden door opens to reveal a hulking Golem. Clad in an expensive, tailored, gray pinstripe suit, the clay man's doll-like features mimic a melted vintage Halloween mask.

His, and I use that pronoun loosely, features are runny, and hollow black circles masquerade as eyes. Grunting, he moves his bulk to the side to allow me entrance. Tamping down the urge to shudder, I begin the descent into the underbelly of the popular spot. Inanimate objects brought to life creep me out. *Give me the actual dead anytime.* Tingling hands and a plummeting core temperature hit as my instincts flare to life. A familiar pulsing energy identifies the dead ahead as vampires. While not alive, they didn't have the same flatline feel as a zombie or ghost.

The bottom level is set up like a swank mansion from the 1950s. Wingback chairs and round tables were placed around the room. In the back-corner section, I slip behind a pair of black curtains into an alcove. A group of men who look as if they stepped off a cover of *GQ* sit around a massive wooden table. A fire crackles in the fireplace below a massive mantle. Dense with the power in the room, the air is stifling. Walking feels more like swimming through water made of energy.

A brunet vampire with long hair pulled back into a sleek ponytail, and delicate features offset by icy, amber-colored eyes devoid of emotion, frowns. His slender fingers tighten on his lion head cane. "You didn't tell me anyone else would be joining us." Disapproval and disdain drips from every word he utters. Clearly, he thought he had the upper hand.

"I prefer the art of surprise. It keeps things honest," his client, my boss for the night, Bronson Allerton, says. The white-blond-haired man with an angular face, sharp jawline, and deep-set dark blue eyes that could freeze a polar bear curves his thin lips up into a smirk. The vampire scowls heavily.

On his right, another chestnut-haired vampire with an aquiline nose, broad forehead, and pricy gray suit wrinkles his nose. "Necromancer." His vampires shift in their seats, watching their master for cues.

"You didn't think I'd do business unprotected, did you, William?" Branson asks slyly. "He's here to even the playing field."

The natural skill that labeled me an outcast back home and a freak among my own kind has proved to be lucrative in the freelance sector. With one foot in the world of the living and the other in that of the dead, I consider myself an equal opportunity contractor. For the right price, I'll work for any supernatural race. I take my spot, holding up the wall behind Bronson's side, and extended my powers to encompass us. Fun factoid, the affinity I have for all things dead, makes me, and select others of my choosing, impervious to vampires' potent mental powers.

Unable to be compelled, my client is now free to do business confidently. Being a blocker ain't the most exciting gig, but it'll help get rid of those pesky pink letters littering the coffee table like decor. Zoning out, I settle in for a lengthy wait.

Rubbing my eyes, I wince. A burning sensation accompanies blurred vision. It's like I've been doused with chlorine. Slowly climbing the stairs to my front porch, I blink rapidly as the sun blinds me with its majestic splendor in shades of peach and violet. I sneer at the picturesque scenery too cheery for my current disposition. *I'm like a vampire with none of the perks.* Weary from the hours, constant work with not enough pay, and overload of political crap, I latch onto the energy my wards provide once I move inside. Plopping onto the black leather couch, I pull out my cell. I lived to work another day, time to reward myself with some Uber Eats.

Because it's a celebration of life, I order a steak dinner, medium-rare—I have some standards—a loaded baked potato, and a wedge salad, paid for courtesy of my newly replenished bank account. Ignoring my growling gut, I help my funds dwindle again by paying off the plethora of past-due bills. With the persistent collectors satiated, I turn my attention to the voice mail message on my phone.

Mom. Her name on my call log alarms me. Nothing short of disaster or death would cause my maternal incubator to contact me. *I need a drink and a full stomach before I can even try to tackle this.* Suddenly, I'm feeling more like I'm fifty-five. The doorbell rings. *Thank you, Zach Morris, for saving me with the bell.* Licking my lips, I can already taste the bourbon burning a path

7

down my throat into my belly as I open the door for a pimple-stricken youth bundled in a black wool coat and a beanie of the same shade.

For a moment, I long for the innocence that comes with the ignorance of magic. The supernatural gives powers, but it also complicates the hell out of everything. Giving the driver a healthy tip, I retreat back into my blackout curtain, sun-proof lair, and eat the food. Washing everything down with the brown alcohol with notes of caramel and burnt sugar, I pretend it doesn't taste like sawdust thanks to my worries.

I swear my past could ruin a trip to the happiest place on Earth. Cutting my meat, I focus on chewing to nourish my lankier rather than lean frame. The weight loss took my appearance from early twenties to teens. They liked to say 'Black Don't Crack' … I see them, and raise them an 'Asians Don't Age'. Once you add the magical element, I counted on being carded well into my fifties.

Done stalling, I push away the white Styrofoam to-go box. Avoiding problems never makes them any easier to deal with. Slouched back against the chair, I lift the cell phone that feels like a heavy brick and press the appropriate code. Tense, I wait to hear the voice that stopped bringing comfort when I was five and first came into my magic.

"Ezra. Your Aunt Hisa died in her sleep last night.

The funeral will be in three days, followed by the reading of her will the next morning. I know the two of you shared a bond."

Bond. A nice way to say we were both afflicted by the same magic that turned us into castaways. More mother than aunt, Hisa took me under her wing, nurturing, and frequently reminding me our powers were a gift to be celebrated despite everyone's obvious aversion and fear. Meanwhile, my own mother kept her sister at a distance and watched me like a suspected turncoat.

Back then, witches were still recovering from the war with vampires. Distrust and paranoia were at an all-time high. Being intimately entwined with death turned me into a child to be ashamed of. No matter how hard I worked at impressing her, I never truly stood a chance. Fifteen years my mother's senior, Hisa was the oldest of the four siblings in the Zaan family.

Born in a time of war, Hisa opted out of procreation herself, for fear of passing down her death magic. Once, in their homeland, they'd been revered for their power. Speaking to those who died and settling restless spirits was a time-honored tradition in her tiny village in Japan. Here in this new world, things were different, distorted, unappreciated. There was no honor. Spells were sold at the highest price to the one with the deepest pockets. Even as some of their kind came together, they watched one another with wary eyes, interacting with vampires as necessary. I never missed the tension once I left Snoqualmie.

Life was calmer in Seattle. *Lonelier too. Better to be alone in a town full of strangers than alone in a home full of family.* Nothing cut deeper than rejection from the group of people who were supposed to love me unconditionally. Straight A's, advanced magical powers, none of it led me to the things I craved most. I worked myself to death, trying to step out of my younger brother's shadow. Until her ...

No. I suffered enough tonight. That wasn't a rabbit hole I could afford to go down on top of everything else.

Tomorrow, I'll drive back home for Aunt Hisa. I owe her that and so much more. Someone who loved her absolutely needs to be present as she's laid to rest.

Blinking to lubricate my dry eyes, I can only stare at the gray-green historic home. The three bedroom, two and a half bath dwelling was a safe haven growing up. A wooden bench with the hand-sewn cushion rests against the wooden trellis covered in fat white flowers as big as my fist. The moonflowers put on a show as they strain toward the light source shining down on them through the rectangular wooden structure they were wrapped around.

Holding the wheel tight, I linger in the car, reluctant to enter the place that held so many joyful memories. *Will it feel like an empty shell without her presence?* Exhaling, I pry my Kung-fu grip from the cylindrical object, and rip off the Band-Aid, stepping from the car. A gust of wind brings the spiced wildflower scent downwind. Inhaling, I reacquaint myself with the smell of home as I travel up the brick pathway.

Sitting on the bench, I close my eyes and let the past sweep me up in its embrace. There was good be found here in Snoqualmie, regardless of how fleeting. Memories of conversations held over tea in the evenings and magic lessons flooded my brain.

"Finally, my boy has come home." The gentle voice soothes and pains me.

"Aunt Hisa." Her name is a whisper on my lips. I open heavy lids and stare into the dark gaze of the fully formed apparition seated beside me. Fact, working with the dead doesn't save me from the sting of loss. My chest tightens. Sandalwood and rose waft from her. Her delicate, heart-shaped face is now wrinkle-free and framed by thick, jet-black hair that tumbles down her back. She can't be more than thirty-something at best. A white dress drapes her petite frame and flows to the ground, reminding me of the muses from *Hercules*.

"Welcome back, Ezra." Her wide grin is off-putting.

"How could it be a happy occasion when you're no longer here, Aunt Hisa?"

"I've merely transformed into a different kind of being. You and I know better than most, energy never dies. It changes."

"While I can't fault your logic, I still miss having you here in the physical world."

She smiles sadly. "It's the circle of life turning. We adapt and continue on. The time has come for you to take your place as my heir."

I flinch. "What place? They cast me out. Not that I ever belonged. They all made sure I knew that from the minute I was old enough to understand what it meant to wield death magic."

"And yet it does not change the things you, and *only you,* are capable of doing. The light needs the dark to remain balanced. They work in tandem. Our family has become imbalanced as I aged. It's why your powers are so great to compensate."

"I will do what you ask me out of respect, but don't expect miracles with them, Oba. They are who they've always been." Used to the imposed distance between my immediate family, I don't dare hope for anything more. Hope can give wings, but it also decimates and destroys. Survival beyond the next few days it'll take to settle the estate is my immediate endgame. Stay cool, fulfill duties, and get the hell out of dodge before the demons I've managed to keep at bay resurface.

"Things rarely go to plan around here," Oba drawls. "I felt a shift in the air before I transcended. Can you sense it?"

Going still, I tap into the land and its natural vibrations. A subtle tremor travels from deep within the earth. My flesh crawls at the *wrongness*. Power radiates from the tendrils, seeking to take root in the soil. Stunned, I come back to my body, chilled. Shivering, I expect to see a cloud formed in front of my mouth as I breathe.

"What is that?"

She shook her head. "It's old magic, ancient and unfamiliar to me."

"From what? A spell?"

"Perhaps." She tilts her head. "It feels directly connected to the elements. The old powers have been awakening at a distressing rate since you've gone. Witches and vampires alike are rallying, striving for a future of peace and cooperation."

I snort. "Surely, no one is buying into their naïve plans."

"They've put their words into actions. The councils meet once more. A series of third-party groups comprised of vampires and witches are working together, smoothing the rough waters. Some believe a war is coming, and in order to win, we'll have to stand as one."

"And the other witches buy this?" I ask, truly intrigued. *Have things changed so much since I've been gone?*

"They're listening."

"As interesting as local politics have become, I have no dog in this fight. Whatever the stance our family decides to take has no bearing on me outside of this town. My life is in Seattle. That isn't going to change." Standing, I remove my keys from my pocket and unlock the front door.

"It's late, and I need sleep to deal with everyone in the morning." I stop in the doorframe. "Do you want me to tell them I can see you?"

She pauses before sighing. "Not yet." She shakes her head. "It's too soon." Like so many things between us, it will remain our secret.

"Then I'll keep it to myself." Speaking with the ghost of my recently departed aunt, I manage to shake off the vestments of loneliness that plague me in this town. *Too bad it won't last.* Turning away from the fading apparition, I retrieve my things. *Sleep.*

CHAPTER TWO

The rich scent of chrysanthemums meld with the light, floral tones of the white lilies arranged in an elaborate display around Hisa's photo at the altar. An array of white blooms creates a virtual garden. Precisely positioned in varying sizes, they form a floral wave. The water theme symbolizes the ebb and flow of life. Nodding my approval, I shove my hands my pockets. Mother's cool magic brushes past me. I turn. The door of the church opens. It gives a cool burn that can cut one to the quick, much like her sharp tongue. Despite her social standing in the magical community, Aunt Hisa was given the lion's share of magical abilities. Our family ruler is decided by age and skill set, not gender. Keeping my gaze fixed on the photo, I hold my tongue. *Let her make the first move.*

"I don't need to remind you that we need to present a united front during this process, do I?"

Same shit different day.

"Hello, Mother. Don't worry. I haven't forgotten the Zaan rules while I've been away. I'll abide by them for Oba's sake. However, it'd be unwise to mistake my show of respect for anything more."

She sucks her teeth. "Why must you be so disagreeable and rude?"

"I return what I receive," I reply calmly, deflecting her attempt at mind games.

I face her for the first time in years. Her heart-shaped face is mostly smooth, and her hair remains the same coal black. Blunt bangs and a short bob highlight sharp cheekbones. Narrowed almond-shaped, brown eyes stand out against clear skin. Thin lips press into a straight line that matches the aura of displeasure she exudes.

"You'll find me a changed man."

"So, I've heard."

"Nice to know you kept up with me. I admit I'm surprised you cared enough to do that."

"You *are* my child." Only she could make that statement sound like an insult.

"People only exist for you when they serve a purpose,

Mother. Once they prove themselves to be of little or no value, they become background noise." Her eye twitches, but she has enough decency to remain silent. We both know there were no lies in my previous statements. "Let's make nice, shall we? I'll play my part. Then we'll go our separate ways until another unfortunate event brings us back together."

She studies me warily. "You may have been born from my body, but you were always more her child."

"Oba understood me and treated me like a person instead of a pariah. All children want to be loved and accepted. It might shock you, but that's not hard to do. Fortunately, for both of us, I realized you're not capable of offering those things to me. I won't be expecting them from you any longer. The flowers are beautiful. She'd be happy with this layout. If you'll excuse me, I'm going to walk the perimeter and make sure things are as they should be."

Turning on my heels, I walk away, leaving her behind me. Back straight, and head high, I double check the lily and baby's breath pew decorations that stand for earth and air, along with the vases with floating white candles that represent water and fire. To nonmagical beings, it will be an unusual yet beautiful gesture that suits the woman with the green thumb and love of nature. Others will understand the symbolism.

"Be careful not to sink to their level." I peer up at my Oba's spirit. "You're no longer the ill-tempered youth trapped by lack of choices."

"And here I thought I'd done well," I mumble.

"You want to make me proud? Show them the man you've become."

"I will, Oba."

Chaotic energy sweeps in as my brother approaches. *No wonder she warned me.* Ari Zaan, the golden child. The little prince to my demon, he could never do wrong. Constantly held up as an example of everything I could never be, he'd quickly become the bane of my existence. Our differences pitted us against one another before we could consciously decide how to proceed with our relationship.

His five-foot-eleven frame appears in the doorframe. He stalks in like he owns the place. Diamond cufflinks wink in the buttonholes of his expensive black suit. Our dark gazes lock, and he moves forward like a great cat who's caught sight of his prey.

I used to let my anger get the best of me. No one crawled under my skin and pressed all the right buttons like him. A pro at manipulating my emotions, he made me feel more puppet than boy growing up. *I've learned patience since then.* Despite his height, Ari felt smaller. The life of luxury and indulgence left him soft.

I can see weakness in his shields, and an openness susceptible to magical attacks. A special kind of strength is gained when you stay hungry and work for everything you have.

Ari's magic shoots forward, assessing me. He stops short, and his eyes dilate. "You've changed, Ezra."

"Time will do that to you, *little* brother." Flexing my magical muscle, I smirk when Ari tenses. "We're here to handle family business. I don't want your spot on the throne."

"As if you could take it." Ari sneers.

"So confident." I search the funeral home for lingering spirits. "Are you sure *this* is the best place to challenge me?" Focusing my powers, I allow Ari to see the flickering phantoms of disgruntled spirits who refuse to move on. "I think you'll find I have the high ground."

Ari's face pales, and he gulps.

"Don't mistake the way things used to be for the present. This is the only warning I'll issue. You might reign here in Snoqualmie, but I've spent years in the real world where the only thing respected is power. You've been here so long you believe your own hype. Don't let your mouth write a check your ass can't cash. I'd hate to embarrass you in front of your biggest fan." I look pointedly at Mother.

Ari's eyes move back and forth in his skull rapidly as he takes in all the spirits.

"Run along now." I resend my power.

He hurries away, continuously casting glances over his shoulder. Ari can't see them any longer, but he *knows* they're there. It's enough.

Sandwiched between Mother and Ari, I miss my father's presence keenly. A quiet man with a power to heal, he helped balance Mother's high-strung tendencies and perfection-obsessed persona. With the matriarch mentality, Dad knew from the start he'd take a backseat to family responsibility. It never bothered him. An acupuncturist by trade, he made a living selling herbal remedies along with more magical concoctions. I loved to help him in the store.

The knowledge I gained there came in handy too many times to count over the years. Magic didn't provide a health insurance plan, and I stopped living off my family's dime at eighteen. Petty maybe, but it left me with what little pride I could scrape together after they ousted me over a difference of opinion. Concentrating on the memories being shared about Oba and the impact she had on our community, I endure the service where Mother's feigned grief and victimization nauseate me.

Always at odds, the sisters butted heads and steered clear of each other more often than not. Mother coveted the power her older sister wielded, yet she wanted none of the fall out that came with necromancy. Standing with the others, I move to the front of the church to thank everyone for coming. Oba's body will be cremated tonight. Once it cools down, we'll begin the proper burial rites.

"Thank you for coming." I shake the hand of an elderly man and accept his condolences with a nod. "We appreciate it."

By the time the church empties, my wrist aches, and my face hurts from holding a gracious yet solemn expression.

James, the family lawyer, remains behind as the workers closed the door of the church. The small man pushes his round spectacles back up the bridge of his nose.

"I know this is a bit unorthodox, but there are certain items in Hisa's home that cannot be without a master. So, we will do the reading of the first few pages of her will tonight at her home before the cremation of her body is completed." He smooths the lapels of his jacket down.

"I'll go and get the house ready." I snatch up the exit route.

"Don't get too comfortable there. It might not be yours much longer," Ari calls.

I bite the inside of my cheek to keep from responding to the dig. More sanctuary than a residence, it's the only thing I want, and they all know it. Outside, I loosen the tie becoming a noose around my neck and get into the car. Hitting the gas, I roll down the windows and let the air blow away the anger and resentment rising and lingering inside.

With Dad and my aunt gone, I'm constantly on the defensive with no backup. It sets me on edge. Arriving at the house, I park in the farthest spot under the carport and still. The powerful wards placed around the property waver as they await a new master. As the eldest member of the family, my aunt had been the true matriarch, though she allowed Mother to be the *face* of the operation, a fact Mother resented. *I bet she's chomping at the bit to take her place on the throne.* I'm sickened by the cannibalistic nature of my family.

Quickly changing into black jeans, combat boots, and white button-down with a vest, I feel a bit more like me. The multi-pocketed article of clothing was custom made and spelled to protect, disguise, and retain parts of my power in case I ever run out of reserves. I'm not paranoid. I'm prepared. When you work solo, the top rule for survival is to be one step ahead of the other guy. Sinking into a wooden chair at the head of the massive oak table in the formal dining room, I wait. It doesn't take long before the first car pulls onto the land. Power closes in on them, seeking out any intentions to harm the property or me.

The door opens, and Ari, Mother, and James step inside.

"Already tampering with the wards?" Ari asks.

"They're acting in their own best interest with Oba gone. If it was me, you'd know." I wink.

Ari growls, and I pucker my lips, blowing him a kiss.

"Enough," Mother snaps. "Mr. James, if we could get started, please."

"Of course, Mrs. Zaan." He sits at the table and places his black suitcase on the top. Rolling the combination lock deftly, he cracks open the rectangle that held the orders about to impact our futures.

"We will meet again tomorrow to discuss the less substantial amounts and objects with the others. This, however, needs to be handled delicately." Removing a scroll, he carefully unrolls the white piece of paper. Kanji lines the page.

"I leave my estate and all its content to Ezra Zaan"

My jaw drops. *The entire thing is mine.*

"She wouldn't dare," Mom whispers.

"Absolute power corrupts, and she's seen your vision for the future. She doesn't agree. You may come into more power thanks to the natural order, but I won't help you by adding the magical items she collected to your arsenal," I say.

Mother's nostrils flare, and her eyes flicker with rage. "Even from the grave, she thwarts me."

"You get the power either way. Why do you need anything else?" I ask sharply.

"Because it is mine." Her hand slaps the table. "It always should have been."

"According to you. Neither the universe, nor our ancestors felt that way," I retort. They weigh what's inside each of us.

"What did she ever do with what she was given? Hoard items in her home?" Mother mocks.

"Just because she chose not to broadcast her actions doesn't mean she didn't help others," I point out.

"What do you know?" Ari asks.

"A lot of things. Keep reading, Mr. James." I wave my hand.

"I sensed a change coming on the wind. You'll need Ez at the wheel to survive it. Things, as we know it, are already transforming, and the restructuring is nowhere near complete. Be prepared to adapt or go extinct." James clears his throat and shifts in his seat, clearly uncomfortable being the bearer of tough love.

"Well, that's not cryptic," I mumble.

"What else does she say?" Mother asks, words clipped.

"That you should perform the rituals to transfer the wards to Ezra, and her power to yourself immediately." James stops. "Afterward, you'll invoke ownership of the *Book of the Dead*, Ezra. It's important you be in control before midnight. Left to its own devices, the results could be catastrophic."

"No!" Mother clutches her throat.

I'm shocked into silence. I thought the tome had been

lost, and her ownership was nothing more than an urban legend. Dating back to the time of the Pharaohs, the book possesses potent spells of necromancy and unique magic all its own. The book would place me firmly at the top of the magical food chain. In an instant, my life is harder and easier at the same time.

Setting the wards is more than a walk around the perimeter, calling out to the elements. They're keyed into the very being and require blood to take. Cutting my palm, I bring forth fire in the other hand and allow my blood to drip onto the ground.

By Fire I ward thee:
Guard this space from all ill will,
And those who wish me harm.

Heat engulfs me, blowing back the longish strands of my hair, and drawing a line of sweat onto my forehead. I'd never had manifestations like this. My stickh was with the dead. I continue on, ignoring the newly-formed desert in my mouth.

By Wind I ward thee:
Guard this space from all ill will,
And those who wish me harm.

Droplets of blood disappear into the earth as if the land itself is making a personal contract. The incense burning on the ground releases a thick puff of sage and cedarwood laden smoke. *Maybe it is.* A gust of wind threatens to knock me off my feet as its snags at my jacket with hungry hands. I stumble, swaying like a drunkard. The intensity fades to a gentle breeze, and I right myself.

By Earth I ward thee:
Guard this space from all ill will,
And those who wish me harm.

Rumbling from deep beneath my feet shakes the earth, pitching me back like a horse unexpectedly bucking its rider. Blinking, I find myself ass over kettle. I scramble up, and ride the undulating ground like a surfer on a longboard. Feet planted, I try to flow with the vibrations, instinctively knowing participation is required.

This is my time to prove myself worthy to inherit. Old magic such as this can be nearly sentient. Everything stops abruptly. I fall forward. A mound of dirt piles up beside me. I tense, readying to defend myself from a nocturnal rodent. A tree sapling emerges.

By water I ward thee:
Guard this space from all ill will
And those who wish me harm.

A streak of lightning slashes through the night angrily. A loud clap of thunder vibrates the ground, and the sky opens above me. Cool rain splatters against my clothes, soaking me to the skin. I finish the walk, completing the circuit. Heaviness slams into my chest. I hit the ground, dazed. My vision darkens, and I feel *it*. The house is built upon a ley line. The wards take their energy from the source in exchange for protection.

Storm clouds crowd in as rain continues to come in sideways. Thunder booms, performing a duet with the crackling lightning streaking across the night sky. I can taste the magic in the air. Mother's succession of power has begun. Sitting in the mud, I tilt my head back and open my mouth, swallowing down water to quench my thirst as I try to adjust to the drastic changes my magic has undergone. Energy races inside of me, stretching and reshaping. My skin feels too tight.

Hot and exhausted, I struggle to get my feet back under me. Inside of the house is a reenactment of *Poltergeist*. Things rattle against tables and in cupboards. Random items float in the air. I watch as a candle bobs its way across the room. Rushing wind travels through the house, turning it into a giant wind tunnel. I stare at the couch, slack-jawed. Mother's body hovers in midair, arms crossed over her chest, and hair stands up as if she's submerged in water.

"Is she okay?" I yell to Ari over the noise.

"I don't know." His voice cracks. The sound of fear sets me into motion. Fighting against the concentrated bubble of air surrounding her, I inch closer. Licks of energy strikeout, shocking me. Embracing the pain, I battle my way to her side. Her eyes are wide open but rolled back into her head to reveal pure white. A translucent, multi-colored cocoon surrounds her.

"It's not hurting her." I shake my head as I monitor her. "It's just disconcerting."

A scarlet strand wraps around me and releases a jolt of electricity. Crying out, I hit my knees. Convulsions rock through me. I clench my teeth. The lights flicker off and on. I register my brother's anguished cry seconds before I lose control of my body. Thrust into the backseat of my brain as a new driver takes over, I watch myself like a spectator.

"*Come to me.*" An incessant voice whispers to me with words that are a command. Turning away from my levitating mother, I walk past Ari's prone body on my way to the basement entrance, fully aware this is an astral trip. A glowing white light illuminates the line under the door. Opening the heavy door, I'm stunned by the transformation. White mist creeps up the stairwell like a fog. The source of the white light is a massive Ankh that sits high in the air casting down beams.

"*Come.*"

The room transforms into a hallway straight out of ancient Egypt. Cuneiform etched in the beige stone walls tells a story I can't translate. The air is musty and cool.

Hallways branch off on the left and right, leading to rooms with detailed drawings, and long rectangles that must house sarcophaguses. *I'm in a pyramid.*

Torches line the walls. I turn to the left down a corridor. A dark figure looms ahead on an elevated stone altar. As I draw closer, pointed ears, an elongated snout, a gold head, and onyx headdress with silver ankhs come into focus. The image identifies the being as Anubis, the Egyptian God of Death.

A broad layered wesekh collar laden with precious gemstones drapes from shoulder to shoulder, emphasizing his thick neck. Ornate golden cuffs adorn his forearms, and wrap skirt of the same color reveals powerful thighs and legs. He's like a bodybuilder on steroids, only leaner. His muscular humanoid form and jackal-like face are at odds and seamlessly blended under a glossy black coat of fur-covered skin.

If ever I was going to evacuate my bowels, now would be the time. A black staff with a golden serpent head is clutched in his left hand. Unsure how to proceed, I stop a few feet away from the bottom of the dais.

"Come forward, child of Anubis." I can't help but focus on his wicked sharp teeth as he speaks.

Confused, I wrinkle my brow. *I don't worship him.*

"All who wield the power of death belong to me." His deep voice has a guttural tone impossible to ignore.

My legs move, carrying me with them against my better judgment.

"You are the appointed keeper of my secrets. I expect you to serve me well and protect this book with your life." A large, black tome appears in his hand. Worn with age, the leather is nearly white in spots. Ankhs and scarabs are carved into the cover, but it's the golden Amenta that catches my eye. The upside-down half circle with two lines that resemble blood trails represent the underworld. "It will open only for you." The book floats toward me, and I'm relieved that I won't have to get any closer to the fierce figure.

"Thank you." I bow in respect.

"You'll find ownership of this book to be both a blessing and a curse. Wield its power with care. The balance must be kept above all."

"I understand." I take the book, and I'm yanked back the way I came by an unseen force. Clutching the book to my chest, I close my eyes to block out the blurring scenery around me.

CHAPTER THREE

Zipping up my carry-on, I scan the bedroom for any last-minute items I may have forgotten.

"What are you doing?" Ari appears in the doorway.

"Going home."

"Already?"

I snicker. "I'm sorry, did you think because we've all gotten power upgrades, we're friends? I came here and did this for Oba. I've done that, so it's time to go."

"You're not going to test things out?" Ari crosses his arms over his chest.

"Of course I will ..." moving into the bathroom, I gather my toiletries, "in Seattle."

"You have power now," Ari says, clearly baffled.

"I've always been powerful, Ari."

"Not like this." He shakes his head. "People have to listen to and respect you. Why would you throw it all away when it's finally in your grasp?"

"Because fear isn't love. If you haven't learned that basic lesson, I feel very sorry for you, brother. There's a whole other world beyond this town. Maybe you should visit it occasionally and get some perspective."

"I don't need to go farther than our town when I have everything I need here." He holds out his arms, inflated with his own sense of self-worth.

"Uh, huh. Keep telling yourself that." I nod, ready to leave the shit show that is my family far behind.

"You don't know what you're talking about," Ari scoffs.

"Life's a piece of cake when you're a big fish in a small pond. Maybe stepping outside of that is a little too scary for you," I goad him, amused by how right I am.

His face reddens, and the muscles in his neck flex. "I'm not about to let you get into my head," he snaps, scowling.

"Don't flatter yourself. What you have between your ears isn't worth the effort."

"Boys." Mother's stern tone slices through the tension building between us. "Enough."

"I expect you to be out of here in the next thirty

minutes when I leave. We've all recovered." *And I don't trust you not to snoop.*

"I'm afraid you'll be postponing your trip," Mother purrs.

"Why would I do that?" I narrow my eyes and shift my weight.

"We've been summoned." She holds up a letter sealed with black wax.

"By who?"

"The council. The magic we did the other evening was potent. They must've sensed it."

I don't buy it for one second. "They knew Aunt Hisa died."

"Yes, and now they want to see where they stand, and how much stronger we are. I know because it's the same move I would make if the roles were reversed. Know your enemies and your allies."

"And here I thought everyone was getting along so well," I say sarcastically.

"We are. This is them covering their bases."

"I'll leave the two of you to handle that. I haven't been an active member of this family for years," I say, not about to get pulled into the Zaan black hole.

"If you don't show up given your history, it'll be perceived badly." Her voice is high and sharp.

I shake my head. "I'm not a show pony you can take out and flaunt when the mood suits you."

"You're a part of this family, regardless of if you'd like to be or not."

"No." I ball my fists at my side. "You don't get to do that."

"What are you talking about?" she asks waspishly.

"Pretend like you didn't push me away and alienate me. Clearly, you were the one who had a problem with *me* being in this family."

"You chose *them* over your family."

And the skeletons are falling out of the closet.

I don't bother arguing with her perception. She'll see it how she pleases. "You gave up on me long before that happened. Did you expect me to remain on the sidelines in some sort of stasis forever, begging for scraps of attention and affection? Everyone has a breaking point. I reached mine and found what I needed elsewhere."

"You fell under *her* spell and forgot everything you were taught." The ugly wound rips open. Puss explodes, putrid and cloying as she spews words.

"Oh no, I remembered the loneliness, humiliation, neglect. Should I continue?"

"This," she waves the sealed envelope in the air, "is bigger than our petty grievances."

I give a dry laugh. "That is where you're wrong. This is the empire you lust after. I couldn't care less. So, you can deal with this on your own. The same way you've been doing for nearly twenty years."

The door to the room slams shuts.

"Don't you think you're a little old for tantrums?" I ask, unimpressed by her theatrics.

"I am more than your mother. I am the leader of this family. You will obey me."

"You can try to force me, but it'll just end up making us both uncomfortable." The power Aunt Hisa bequeathed puts me neck and neck with her power level, and my sense of family loyalty is weak and watered down. "Funny, you just acquired new powers, and already you're using them to try and control others. Classy."

"A queen rules when subjects obey."

"No. A good queen would have subjects who respected and admired her enough to want to follow her. You never understood that. It's why your power ended up divided." Disappointed in the ways she hasn't changed, I strengthen my resolve to leave. "Our family has power and respect, but in the grand theme, we're small. No one other than you will care if I'm not present."

"Eyes are always watching and waiting for an opportunity."

"For what? I'm estranged, halfway across the country, and not interested in the local politics."

"Don't you understand you have to fill the hole your

Oba left?" The air around us prickles against my skin as
the ozone rises.

"Did you read some fine print I didn't see on the will?
This is all mine to do with as I see fit." I thump my chest.
"Me. Oba pointed out, specifically, she didn't agree with
your views and the policies she knew you'd want to en-
force. You don't get to decide this. I'm finally useful, and
you pull my string to make me dance like a marionette.
I'm smarter than that, Mother."

"Then act like it." Her cheeks grow pink as the cool
façade slips.

"And how do you propose I do that?"

"By acting like you care about what happens to this
family."

Swallowing the caustic words that threaten to crash
over me like a tsunami-size wave ready to swallow me
alive, I opt for silence. After everything she put me through,
she doesn't deserve my emotions. I lock them down like
a fort on high alert, turn, and pick up the handle of my
suitcase. Rolling it behind me, I slip on my sunglasses and
concentrate on placing one foot in front of the other.

"Don't you walk away from me."

Ignoring her high-pitched squeal, I continue. Doors
open and slam shut. A picture slants on the wall, and I
pause. *This is my house now. I have the high ground.*
Pausing in mid-step, I turned to look over my shoulder.

"I'd appreciate it if you'd respect my home. If you can't control yourself, I suggest you leave."

Her jaw drops. *You taught me how to play the game well, Mother.* "Things have changed. For the record, I *do* care about our legacy. What I don't care for is pettiness and inflated ego. When we can't set aside the shallow surface, nothing worthwhile is actually accomplished. Oba has been talking about the change happening in the community for a while now. It intrigued me. The world they're trying to build is one I'd be interested in being a part of. Then I come back, and it's like you've been living in a time capsule because nothing has changed. You've just gained the power and prestige you always wanted. What is it you really want from me? If it's to turn me into a *yes man,* you should know by now it'll never happen." Studying her face, I wait.

Her lower lip quivers and her dark eyes turn glossy. She balls her fists, and the ruckus stills. *Is this how we're going to leave things after so much time apart?* After so many years trying to fill the distance between them and fix the gnawing emptiness my childhood left me, I don't have it in me to extend a hand or make this any easier on her.

"You to take your proper place within the family."

I close my eyes. If I squint, it's so close to hearing what I needed to. But in the ways that mattered most, I see it as a cheap cop-out. The little boy in me silently begs me to bend the knee. The adult knows better.

"Why?" I prolong the conversation, to give her a chance to show me anything that would make me stick my neck out again. *Now is your time.* My heart rate increases as I hold my breath. *This time it could be different.*

"Because it's time."

Deflated like a kicked puppy, I exhale slowly. "Goodbye, Mother." Turning away, I blink back the allergic reaction agitating my dry eyes. The distance to the door felt longer, but I manage it regardless.

Stepping out onto the front porch, I allow myself a moment to choke back the emotions swirling around in my stomach and threatening to climb up my throat. Back in control, I walk to my car, unsurprised when I receive no further resistance. Hitting the button on my key fob, I unlock the sedan and open the trunk. As I toss my bag in the trunk, I vow to come back unannounced on my own. They're in for a rude awakening once I get far enough away for the wards to make them uncomfortable.

Keyed in to its owner, it responds in kind. Oba was a lot more zen about the family situation than I was. They'll find themselves increasingly uncomfortable until they are forced to flee. Maybe my friends from the other side will pay a visit to welcome them. The benign spirits I helped or interacted with often tend to follow me around and haunt the places I frequent. I don't mind them. They can be quite beneficial. The wards flare, and I tense in response.

The pull of the dead told me they are not of the living. *Vampire?* Perhaps they've come to pay their respects? My Oba had friends from all walks of life. Steeling myself to deal with the politics of the undead, I fix my face into a pleasant, unaffected mask and walk my way down to the edge of the property line to greet them in person. The brown-skinned female is unrecognizable from this distance.

When I get close enough to make out her features, I balk. The blood rushes from my head. I blink to try to clear away the hallucination in front of me. *This can't be happening.* The oval faced burned into my brain is still surrounded by voluminous, kinky, brownish-black hair with a medium curl pattern. Her snub button nose is every bit as adorable, and her wide lips are just as pink and plump. I hate myself for the memories that bubble to the surface, conflicting with the intense loathing I automatically experience.

"Waylon?" Disbelief colors my mind. The one person whose relationship is more complicated than mothers had shown up like it was a daily occurrence. I haven't seen her in over a year, and that separation wasn't long enough.

"Hello, Ez."

I hate the cream dress with shoulder pads and the way its clingy material accents her slender frame with its tempting curves. She's still remaining true to her 80s aesthetic. Anger explodes. My power responds, bursting forth like a heat-seeking missile. The energy is dispersed by a magical shield surrounding her with an audible crack. Flinching, she grimaces.

"I anticipated that. Henceforth, the magical protection."

Finding a loophole, I fling her a hundred yards away from my door. This backstabbing temptress ripped my heart from my chest and humiliated me. I gave up everything to be with her, and she turned her back on me when I needed her most.

"How dare you show up like this?" The words are venom aimed at her like a sharp needle. I want them to penetrate her skin and flow into her veins, so she can feel a portion of the pain she inflicted so easily.

"This is bigger than you and me."

"According to you, that's not a hard task. Get away from my property." I continue to sling blasts of power her way. If she won't listen, I'll force her hand.

She dodges, rolling like a fighter on the mat. "That's not fair," she yells over the wind I've kicked up.

"Who are you to talk to me about fairness?" Lightning

streaks the sky. "I can make you leave." I take hold of her will, freezing her into place.

Her eyes threaten to bulge from her skull. "Stop this." Turned in the 90s, she's a baby vampire. Her resistance isn't the same as that of an older vampire.

"You're not wanted here, Waylon," I say coldly.

"Stop. I'm here on behalf of the Cortez Court."

The admission changes everything.

"What?" I lower my hands.

"They sent me to speak with you and personally invite you to the Coalition council meeting. We felt blindsiding you with my presence would be a bad start."

What the hell would the most powerful collective of open-minded supernatural want with me, or her? Last I checked, she was on the opposite side of the spectrum.

"Why aren't you with your *family*?" I ask, thinking of the dark-hearted group who'd stolen the girl I fell in love with and turned her into a monster.

"I woke up and realized they weren't who I wanted to be."

"How fortunate for you," I drawl, unimpressed by her enlightenment.

"I was young, Ez."

"You were old enough to know better. If you're seeking sympathy, you've come to the wrong person."

Ducking her head, she glances down. *You should feel bad.* "They were different times."

"So are these. I've been warned about the changes. Fortunately for us both, I won't be there."

"You should really listen to what I have to say."

"That ruined my life once. I'll pass." I turn away.

"We know you inherited the *Book of the Dead*."

I twitch. Her words force my hand. I have to listen now. "How would you know that?"

"There's been visions, along with other things. Lazarus would like to speak with you alone before the meeting starts."

Once again, she's got me by the balls. The powerful vampire isn't one to be dismissed. My hands itch to wrap around her long, elegant neck.

Crouched on the ground, she looks up at me. "Can I deliver his message now?"

I want to reject her, and allow her to go home to her people empty-handed, defeated, and broken. Remembering the powerful vampire in charge of the clan, I quickly squash the ideal.

Moving slowly, she shrugs off her backpack and re-moves a black envelope with a red seal with a regal C. Disgusted by the thought of moving any closer, I use my power to retrieve the paper square and direct it into my hand. She's an infection I can't risk. First loves have a way of getting under your skin and burrowing so deep you can never remove all traces. Breaking the seal, I pull out the letter.

"We've seen signs that the Night Hunt will be reprising soon. Our seer saw you coming into power and being a pivotal part of our survival."

The words blur. Panic detonates inside of me like a bomb. Images of broken bodies, ashes of vampires, and carcasses of what were once witches drained dry of life fill my head. We all know our history. My stomach cramps. My plans are effectively canceled for the foreseeable future. Right now, betrayal will have to take a back seat to survival.

I try not to peer at Waylon out of the corner of my eye. I feel like I'm in the car with a dangerous creature that could turn on me any second. I suppose in the most literal sense I am. Physical pain I can survive. Emotional has always been my Achilles tendon. I don't care for much, but when I do, it's to the point of stupidity. Everyone has to have a weakness. This is mine.

"Are we going to do the whole ride like this?" she asks.

"Silently? I sure as hell hope so."

"Because the sound of my voice is painful?"

"Yes, Waylon. It kind of is. This is me forcing myself to be civil. You're lucky you can't hear the conversation going on in my head."

"It's been years."

"Time doesn't fade everything." I grind my teeth. "If you have to talk, fill me in on what I need to know. There's no way this happened out of nowhere with no signs."

"No, but from what I've heard, they didn't tie the breach to the Night Hunt. We had darker entities force their way through the breach. They committed crimes that drew the attention of humans, and clean-up had to be done fast."

For that to happen, the barrier between the two worlds has to be thin. Cracks that big couldn't be easily sealed. They were like leaks in a dam—as soon as you plugged one up, another appeared and ruined the integrity of the structure. Unlike a dam, magical walls weren't so easily restored or maintained.

What took clans of witches working together to fortify could not be so easily maintained or recreated in times of strife and mistrust. It would truly take everyone coming together to do damage control. With the Hunt on the table, there's no time for posturing. Mountains move, pride is swallowed, and disdain becomes well-hidden when matters of life or death are on the line.

Despite my less than stellar upbringing, I loved

growing up in Snoqualmie. Tucked away from the hustle and bustle of larger cities, a quick drive away, the city has a laid-back vibe. Nature is allowed to be queen here with the large, majestic trees free to grow as tall as they saw fit, and large swaths of land between homes. I can't help but admire the greenery that hasn't changed. Full of folks who depend on nature and secrecy to survive, the city ensures it has plenty of both. Being surrounded by people who had things that needed to remain hidden had been comforting. We were all in the thing together, and getting out alive and free to live life on our own terms had been the main goal.

Certain areas provided that in Seattle, but it hadn't been quite the same.

"And what do your court and the witch families think about what's been occurring?"

"The Coalition has seen a lot of movement recently. Vampires and witches are mingling and forming meaningful relationships at a rate unlike we've seen before. Some people think it's long overdue, and others aren't so …" she pauses, "open-minded."

I snicker. "Oh, I bet." There are those who are too holier than thou to mingle with *common* witches, so I can imagine how they feel about the new integration program. Bigotry was the same across the board. Being the black sheep myself, I knew how much separation and isolation hurt. It all but pushes us toward the darkness that claims with its offer of acceptance. Once you fall into its clutches, the results remain with you for the rest of your life, provided you can ever get away long enough to gain clarity. I'm not Obi-Wan, but I've seen the path the dark side takes you on. I knew early on I never wanted to end up like Anakin. It's why I left.

Starting a new life trumped starving for life in a familiar setting. Things were never great between me and my mother. I'd be the first to admit that. Waylon was the tipping point that sent us barreling downhill like a snowball. Denying it wouldn't make it any less true. I sneak a peek at the woman who'd been an insta grenade and blown my life and my heart to pieces. She still talks with her hands and her face. While her tone can remain neutral, her face will tell it all. *Or is this an act for my benefit?*

My gut clenches. I hate this situation as a whole. The shackles of duty chain me up to hell on earth every time. It's the curse of being a Zaan. I do a double-take at the group walking on the side of the road. They look like flesh and blood but aren't. I frown. Ghosts don't usually trick my eyes so easily.

"I wonder what they're doing out here," Waylon mumbles.

"You see them?" I ask.

"Yes?"

Braking, I pull over to the side of the road.

"What are you doing? We need to meet—"

"Those are spirits, Waylon. You shouldn't have noticed they were there. I'm going to go find out why." Unbuckling my seatbelt, I climb out of the car and walk the short distance to meet the group. Dressed in modern-day clothing, they're as fresh as a daisy and completely unbothered or ignorant to their undead status.

"Do you need help?" I ask cautiously.

"I think we're beyond that." The dark-haired male, with brown eyes and a jagged scar above his eyebrow, has a deep baritone. Dressed in a pair of navy slacks and a matching shirt with a white name patch, proclaiming his as Scott, he looks enough like the boy and girl for me to assume he is the father. Which makes the willowy woman with dishwater blonde curls and a solitaire diamond with a matching band on her ring finger his wife. He wraps an arm around her shoulder. From the sound of it, he at least knows they're dead.

"There is a place for you to go."

"We were following the light, and then it winked out, and left us stranded."

My eyes widen. "Winked out?"

"Yes. It flickered, and then things blurred and we ended up on the side of the road beside the car accident."

The walls are thinning between dimensions, and it's interfering with the proper order.

"I think I can help." Reaching out, I find an older member of the formerly living club and call them to me. A woman appears, dressed in a gown from the early 1900s.

"Pardon me, sir," she says huffily.

"This family is lost and seeking the light. Have you seen it?" I ask.

The pinched face woman in the oversized hat, slanted slightly with white plumage to offset the plum that matched her large dress, twitters. "Hallowed ground is yet to be disturbed. The local cemetery."

"Thank you, madame. I'm sorry to disturb your slumber. Things are not as they should be here. We're working on it." I bow.

"The huntsmen approach. We can feel them clawing at the thinning walls. It's been so long since they were allowed their freedom, we fear the carnage they will leave behind. Many of us have family that remains here."

I nod. "Assure the others we are aware, and coming together once more to put them back in the netherworld where they belong."

She curtseys. "If you will follow me, I shall lead you to the light." The woman straightens before she sets off, walking like a regal queen who expects her people to follow.

Knowing they were in good, if conceited, hands, I make my way back to the car. Climbing inside, I push the speed limit. Things are worse than I thought. There are spirits who wait eons to take advantage of a situation such as this one. Freed, they'll make a bad situation catastrophic.

"Where did those spirits go?" Waylon whispers.

"Toward the light. They were lost."

"Why is it I could see them?" She fiddles with her seatbelt. "I've never had that happen before."

"The walls between planes are weakening with the coming of the huntsmen. It's turning the natural order on its head. I spoke to another ghost who confirmed it."

"What does that mean?"

"If we can't get a handle on it, the huntsmen will be the least of our worries. Dark spirits have been locked away for a reason. If they start getting free …"

I shake my head, not willing to put the thoughts out into the universe. Words have power.

CHAPTER FOUR

We pull in front of the The Parlor. The successful pizzeria and brewery act as a front for the supernatural dealings going on in the basement. A neutral zone, it caters to all types and plays host for major mixed company council events. The three-story glass and metal monstrosity looms ahead. With outdoor seating on both levels and a wide variety of brews to try, it's a popular spot in our small town. Table and bench seating fill the space on the inside.

"We'll go around the back," Waylon says. Neither of us moves a muscle. How do you act gracious to be somewhere you never wanted to be in the first place? I don't know, but I've always been good at thinking on my feet.

"Should we roll for it?"

Waylon's words take me back to the start of the best and worst thing that would ever happen to me—our first meeting.

The Hyatt, 1999 Gamer Con

"You never told me how you managed to get your mom to agree to let you loose for the week," Aim says as we leave our hotel room to mingle for a bit. All our matches are scheduled for later this evening, so we're free to enjoy the festivities the convention has to offer.

"I didn't. I bypassed the Dragon Queen and went to the King, who promptly declared all work and no fun will ruin his best assistant who deserved a break. She can find fault in many things, but my work ethic has never been on that list."

"Thank God for Mr. Zaan," she says.

"I second that. My dad is the best."

Taking the elevator down to the first floor, we flash our badges as we walk through to the merch section. After staking out what we wanted the first day, we're back to fork over our hard-earned cash. I veer to the Buffy bonanza, while she moves over to the table with the Sailor Moon merch.

"Did you get what you wanted?" she asks.

I shake my black bag at her, and we continue to explore at a more leisurely pace.

"I figured now would be the time to bulk up for the room decorating coming."

"Are you excited?" I ask.

She shrugs. "I don't know. I mean, I know your college is a fantastic school, but being an hour and half away seems so far."

"Hey. I'll be out there to bug you all the time, and you're close enough to come home on weekends if you want."

"Yeah." She scowls. We've gotten so used to always having each other. It's spoiled us.

"Come on." I bump my shoulder against hers. "Let's go check out the competition."

The bloodthirsty gleam enters her eyes and she takes off at a fast clip. I follow easily, and we enter the massive ballroom packed with tables. People are dressed in casual clothes as well as elaborate costumes. I recognize a lot of them from previous years. Taking the time to observe their play, I see many have improved, while others have stayed the same. Tabletop gaming is more than the luck of the roll. It's also about strategies and reading people.

"Do you see her?" Aim asks.

"Who."

"The girl right there in the dress." She nods her head

toward a curly-haired, slender girl with a pretty face. "She's the one to beat. I've watched her play in the local tournaments and she's made a pretty penny winning nonstop."

"Witch?" I guess.

"No one's sure. She's got a potent blocking spell going."

"Interesting. She sounds like a challenge."

"You've been out of the competitive circuit for most of the year. Are you sure you're up for it?"

"You wound me." I click my tongue. "Best friends are supposed to raise each other up."

Aim smiled. "I just thought it'd be nice for you to have a bit of healthy competition for once. You've dominated this thing for the past two years."

"Mmmhmm. I was there for your Spice Girl stage. I know how you feel about Girl Power."

"I can love Girl Power and you, Ez." She pinches my cheek, and I roll my eyes. Only she would dare pull something like this with me.

Brat knows there's not much I would deny her. She's the sister I never knew I wanted. With her bubbly personality, love for pastels, and pop music, she's an unlikely candidate for necromancy. At first glance, you'd expect her to command the local cheerleading squad, not the dead. Dressed in her Lolita fashion, she's swathed in a

white shirt with puffy sleeves, and a pink and white ruffled creation. The massive bow at the waist emphasizes
her slender frame and makes me smile. You have to love
a person who can be unapologetically themselves.

Meeting online in the AOL group Necro was a life-de-
fining moment that saved me in more ways than I liked to
admit. When we met offline, I knew soulmates could be
platonic. With her infectious smile, positive attitude, and
wicked sense of humor, she was my opposite, but she got
me all the same. When she appeared in my life, I suddenly
found a person who understood me in a way few ever
could.

Unlike my family, hers banded together to deal with
her unusual talent. The first witch to be born in centuries,
she'd taken them all by surprise, revealing a long-forgot-
ten ancestry. Her first experience with the dead was a lot
tamer than my own. At four, she resurrected a group of
fallen butterflies, sending her parents down a rabbit hole.
Uncovering their magical roots and the world that existed beside their own, they carved a space for themselves.

Spending time with the trio gave me hope for a future
full of love, understanding, and a healthy relationship.
Her parents were an ideal couple. A little goofy, but stern
when necessary and always loving, even when they disci-
pline. Her home environment was so different from my
own. I craved it. If Aim minds sharing her family with me,

she never lets on. I don't bother to hide my adoration as I study the changes the months have brought. Between graduation, her prep for college, and my training to become a licensed acupuncturist while I help my father in the store, we haven't spent our usual amount of time together.

Her rail-thin frame has plumped up and she's curvy. Her massive, cat-shaped, dark green eyes stand out against her light brown hair and tan skin in her oval-shaped face. Her thin, pink lips are stretched wide to accommodate her smile.

"You okay, Ez?" she asks semi-seriously.

"Yeah." I nod. "Just realizing how much I've missed you."

"Duh. I'm awesome."

I chuckle, and we continue to walk the room, taking in the games happening at the tables. Sizing up our competition in the *private* section. Magic wielders take tabletop games to an entirely different level. Recreating the scenes like holograms on the table makes things a lot more interesting. My gaze continues to return to the mysterious girl in the gray and white Nintendo game controller covered skater dress. Her magic is strong.

Her monk looks like a tiny figurine as it travels through the forest. Wind blows the monk's white hair around her face, contrasting with her ebony skin, and glowing purple eyes. Her lithe frame is encased in a red and orange form-fitting leggings and top. A red breechcloth with orange trim adds to the aesthetic without hindering her ability to fight, flee, or defend herself. *The monk is well thought out.* While the girl plays cautiously, she never hesitates when it's time to take action.

The player's large, chocolate-brown eyes are fringed with dark lashes that show her every emotion. Her dark brows dip as she leans forward, concentrating hard. Her smallish button nose crinkles.

"Ezra Zaan. Fred Bowen. Your match will begin in ten minutes at table number seven."

Pulling my focus from Waylon, I allow myself to slip into game mode.

"You ready, tiger?" Aim asks playfully.

"Always."

Time, matches, and tables blend together as I play match after match, breaking to use the restroom and re-fuel. In between games, I find Aim, cheering her on when I'm able. I've missed being immersed in this world. Here, everyone has a place. Even outside of the magical matches, we all relate to one another as the misfits and outcasts. I'm not surprised when I find myself seated across from Waylon. Her brash grin and mirth-filled eyes are an enchantment all their own. *Hell of a time to develop a crush.*

"So, we finally meet," she drawls.

I arch an eyebrow. "Has my reputation proceeded me?"

"It has indeed. It's almost a sacrilege to break your winning streak."

"Oooo," is the collective sound from the crowd surrounding us, who eat up the trash talk.

"So confident."

"Totally. I worked my way up the ranks. The big boss is the final one to beat so I can take the crown."

I glance over at a beaming Aminthe who winks.

"I don't know if I'm flattered you see me as the big boss or insulted you believe I'll be defeated so easily."

"Flattered," she assured me. "Don't worry. I promise to buy you bubble tea to help wash down your de-throning."

"May I offer up the same to rinse away the brackish taste of your tears of defeat?"

Her lips twitch upward at the corners. "Game on."

Present

"Ezra?"

"Yeah. I'm ready." I step forward, leaving the past and its memories. Who we were can never be the same as who we are. Life and all it has to throw at us changes us bit

57

by bit until we transform into new beings. The decisions we make determine whether those versions are better or not. I'd like to think my current version is smarter than the young boy hungry for love and acceptance. I learned the hard way; Waylon can't be trusted. Only a fool would walk into the same trap twice. I follow her through the back entrance on the bottom level. The air is cool, and there's a damp smell. We're in the cellar. My shoulders tense as my eyes adjust quickly to the dim lighting.

There's an entire world down here. A section is quartered off to house the brewing, but the rest is tables and chairs that clearly cater to a different crowd. Heads turn as we walk down the wooden stairs. A door opens, and Lazarus steps out first. His navy suit is perfectly tailored with a white handkerchief in his breast pocket and leather shoes that take him over the top. His dark hair is cut short and combed back on the top. I feel cold as his icy blue gaze sweeps over me, sizing me up. I swallow. He's intimidating. The dark aura surrounding him is powerful, more so than his age should allow.

The brown-skinned woman who steps out from behind him with her fuchsia hair earns a grin. Like me, she's a witch that's been looked down on for her unusual preferences. Seeing her on top, and living her best life, is the ultimate middle-finger to the traditionalists in our society who don't want to see anything change.

"Well, hello there, Frida."

"Ezra!" She moves forward and hugs me.

I tense as Lazarus' eyes darken to black and narrow.

"It's good to see you, too. I'd like to live, though, so if you could back up say a foot, I'd appreciate it."

She laughs. "Don't mind him. He glares at everyone."

"Hmph." I take a step back. "Good to see a misfit making good." I bow.

"Stop it." She shakes her head and hooks her arm with mine. "Let's relocate into the office."

Allowing her to guide me, I take in the environment. Business is hopping. Bartenders serve drinks as people talk in intimate groups. My eyes catch the red liquid poured into glasses, too thick to be wine.

"It's responsibly sourced," Lazarus says with a smirk. "Everyone has to eat, Mr. Zaan. We simply provide a social atmosphere where they can partake of their special diet responsibly."

The glint of yellowed eyes draws my attention to another table, where raw meat confirms my suspicions. *Werewolves.* Stepping inside of the office, I feel the wards brush against my skin and find me to be a friend instead of a foe. Like the Tardis, it's bigger on the inside. A smoky glass table is lined with black leather seats. Lazarus gestures to sit.

"We wanted a chance to talk to you in a less formal

situation," Lazarus says. His baritone holds power even I can sense.

"I'm curious to know what you think I can do to help. Calling myself green would be a compliment I don't deserve." Sinking into the chair, I try not to let my nervousness show.

"We understand, and we're sorry for your loss. Your aunt was an exceptional woman."

"Yes, she was," I agree. "Thank you for your kindness. The flowers were exquisite."

He gives a nod of acknowledgment and some of the tension dissipates. The surreal situation has my head spinning. What planet did I land on when I rolled into town? Everything has been turned on its head. *Is Mercury in Retrograde and no one told me?* A vase of pink flowers rests in the center. Waylon takes a seat beside me, and I scowl.

"There's no love lost between the two of you," Lazarus observes.

A straight shooter, I can work with that.

"Our past isn't one I'd choose to revisit voluntarily." I sit in the chair across from him with Frida to his right and Waylon to my left.

"I find matters of the heart are rarely as black and white as we believe them to be."

I bite the inside of my cheek. "With all due respect,

you didn't bring me out here to talk about my love life. I don't mind shooting the breeze, but that's a little too personal for comfort." I glance over at Waylon, whose eyes are suddenly glued to her lap. "Besides, there are two sides to every story, and rarely do they line up exactly."

"I like your honesty. As you're my guests, let me get you something to drink, and then I'll share with you what I know. Are you agreeable to that?"

"I am." Say what you wanted about vampires. Their manners tend to be impeccable. He walks over to the chrome fridge. "Beer, water?"

"Water is fine."

Nodding his head, he doles out bottles for the three of us and we settle in.

"I was around for the last two Night Hunts. The carnage reminded me of the plague days. Bloated bodies lying in the streets with blackened tongues, bruises all over the body, and eyes and faces frozen in masks of terror." He frowns. "Some of the catastrophes that have come through our cities were cover-ups for the savagery of the huntsmen."

I sit up straighter. They've always been whispered about as if mentioning them gave them power. "I've heard rumors of the riders who come, but no one speaks openly about these things in our culture."

"With good reasons. Words have power, and they feed

on the world's misery and waiting for their next chance to begin the hunt." Lazarus shakes his head.

"What are the huntsmen? I never understood how hunters could be immortal? Are they?" I lean forward slightly.

"In a manner of speaking. Hunters were more prevalent in the times when the people still believed and followed the old ways. They weren't so quick to explain away things they've seen using logic, and they raised their children to dispatch of us. They truly believed this was their duty and a holy calling. Righteousness is a dangerous thing. When you think you have high moral ground, there's no telling what you'll justify in the name of the greater good. I've seen good men corrupted and hanged when they were in the right while evil men flourished as they spread lies with their golden tongues. It's all a matter of perspective. You tip the glass one way, and it supports one thing, the other and ... You get the picture."

The sense of history behind his words is telling and unreal. He's seen the rise and fall of nations. I don't even try to hide my admiration.

"After we all came together, their hunts were less and less successful. They'd lost the high ground. Frustrated, they turned to the very thing they hated."

"Magic," Frida whispers.

"Precisely. They bargained with the Unseelie. In

exchange for their service, they are allowed to unleash hell for one period of twenty-four hours. At the place of their choosing."

"And you believe it'll be here?" I guess.

"The unrest has been there for a time. She told you about the previous instances with dark entities?" he asks.

"Yes."

"We thought we solved the problem when we sealed the rogue demons back where they belonged, and hid the object he used."

"What changed?" I ask.

Lazarus glanced at Frida. Reaching out, she twined their fingers, stunning me. They were more than partners in crime.

"It started all over again. Thin spots between the worlds started to pop up and cause interference with the living."

"Expand on that for me," I say.

"Ghosts are more active. Haunting cases have increased as well as possessions. We've felt the darkness growing. It's part of why we've pushed so hard to get everyone speaking to each other and building trust. When we're separate, we're more vulnerable."

"Do you think that's why they've chosen now to resurface?" I question.

"We believe that's part of it. I also think they're being

helped awake." Lazarus sighs. "There's been a lot of dark rituals being performed, and at least one black coven was formed and operating under the noses of their families."

"That's a lot of imbalance in power," I muse. It would explain the disruption that confused the spirits I saw.

"Maybe that's why I saw the spirits on the way here."

Lazarus arches an eyebrow. "You saw ghosts?"

"Yes. We both did actually. It was a family who'd been killed in a car accident. They were following the light to move on when it disappeared. I called in a spirit who said hallowed ground was the only guaranteed safe place these days. She said they smelled the huntsmen on the wind. If you're looking for me to convince my family to help, you're barking up the wrong tree. They'll do it because it's the right thing, and they don't listen to me either way." I shake my head.

"No, but you've inherited your aunt's things. She had the *Book of the Dead*. It was prophesied."

"How do you think that can help you?" I ask.

"We want you to look for information on the hunt and Night Warriors."

"Who?" I ask, wondering if they were talking about the ghosts of the Hawaiian warriors.

"They were a group of fighters who trained to take on the huntsmen. They died out a few years back because the tradition fell out of practice," Waylon explained softly.

"And you sent her why?"

"Because, like it or not, she's someone you know and once trusted, and injured pride is not the same as physical hurt. You were both young, and for the duration of this mission, I'll need you to set your emotions aside."

I grit my teeth. It's easier said than done. "It won't get in the way of what needs to be done."

"Good." He takes a sip from his mug and rests his ankle on his knee.

"That's it?" I inquire skeptically.

He peers at me over the rim of his cup. Placing it gingerly on the table, he shakes his head. "No, it's the beginning. This game is a long one, be prepared to pace yourself. Arming ourselves with knowledge is the way to win this. So much of what is known about the huntsmen is rumor and speculation. We have more than our ancestors did ... access to the book thanks to you, and if they're willing to listen, the Night Warriors. For now, I'd like to keep this between us. Information can be deadly in the wrong hands. As much as I want to present the council as a harmonious, well-oiled machine, we're new and my trust doesn't extend to every member. Politics are a messy business."

"I don't envy you the responsibility," I admit. I pick up my own water bottle and take a small sip.

"For this journey, Waylon will be your partner. Her

loyalty is to me, and she is capable of wielding some magic. It's been shown that you two are meant to work together in order for us to find victory."

"Shown by who?" I ask.

"An oracle." The finality in his tone is a nail in my coffin. Until this is finished, I'm trapped with her.

"And what do you think about this, Waylon? You haven't said much." I angle my body toward her.

"It's my chance to prove myself. I need this. Not just for my new family, but for me. I have things to prove and atone for. This is my chance to right wrongs and move forward. I've been trapped in a cycle that's led me nowhere for far too long." Lifting her head, her face is lined with determination. Her mouth is set into a firm line and her body is tense with energy.

I want her to clarify, but I refuse to get myself involved with her more than I have to. She's like the Earth—her magnetic pull is strong, and once she's got you hooked, you orbit around her. *Not anymore.* I manage a curt nod and stand to fix myself a plate. It's going to be a long afternoon, at least I can endure it on a full stomach.

CHAPTER FIVE

The phrase too many chiefs and not enough Indians, comes to mind as I look around the area where we're set up for the meeting. The council has a few new faces, but the rest remain the same. The Wrights are still their openly racists self with their upturned noses and perma scowls. Their faces are pale beneath their tan skin, and I'm waiting for them to bolt any second. They were from the school that believed vampires were the root of all evil, and beneath us magic-wielding. The fact that Lazarus came from a line that allowed him to create magic himself only made their hate more focused.

"Why have you called us here, Cortez?" Thomas Wright asks.

"You know why," Luke Moore speaks up. His green eyes and wheat-colored hair make him the exact opposite of Thomas in every way. Their opinions, politics, and practices are also on conflicting ends of the spectrum.

Leaning back, I settle in for the show. There's a reason the councils don't have weekly meals. Every family runs differently. Some are matriarchal, others are patriarchal, or a few share their power. It leads to a lot of people believing *their* way is the proper one. As servants of nature, we're meant to be open-minded and accepting, but the truth is people are people whatever abilities they possess.

"If you don't, I suppose that speaks for itself," a male voice says from somewhere in the crowd. Mr. Wright's cheeks grow red.

"I beg your pardon—"

"Gentleman. I think we can all agree there's no time for the infighting." Frida's voice demands silence. The power swirling around her is almost visible as it blows the black hair back from her honey-brown, heart-shaped face. Her deep-set dark brown eyes are sharp. Pursed full lips painted red and curled fingers on her chair play to her impatience. "Things have plagued our town for the past couple of years. All of them had valid reasons which were taken care of for the moment. We've felt the darkness rolling in regardless of the small fires we've been putting out as they ignite. That many strange occurrences point to a shift in the energies that help keep the balance we all strive to maintain. It's our job to stand guardian. Do you disagree?" She studies each of us carefully.

I see the challenge in her steely gaze, daring one of us to speak against her.

I raise my hands, palms up in mock surrender to show her I'm on her side. The Zaans are legends in their own right, but numbers-wise, we're small potatoes. My presence here is unusual and it's been noted.

"Now that we're all on the same page, let's cut to the chase. The signs say the Night Hunt will be upon us soon. I've dreamt it many times. I had hoped these visions would change as we battled the darkness, but I can no longer ignore what I know to be true. I'm not naïve enough to expect you to believe me. My visions are new and I'm young. So, we've brought someone who can speak directly with the dead."

It's showtime.

"Hi. Ezra Zaan, necromancer." I wave.

Thomas sneers. "You want us to trust him? He hasn't been a part of this community for years."

"You must feel the same way about my wife then. She, too, spread her wings and left the community for a time. Is that the case?" Lazarus asks smoothly.

I glance at the ground, to hide the smirk I can't stop from spreading across my lips. He's a clever bastard. I won't add fuel to the fire by openly displaying my humor, but the pompous witch had it coming for years.

"The Zaans have always been powerful and honest. I don't see why there would be any objections to having Ezra here. It's impressive that he left his home and created a life in Seattle where he's highly sought after," Luke says.

The fact that they'd kept tabs on me didn't settle well in my gut. *I'm small potatoes. What did they care?* I don't have an answer, but I sure as hell plan on finding out. Keeping my poker face on, I let the conversation flow around me.

"I'm not opposed," a voice says, starting a round of agreements.

"Fine." Thomas waves his hand dismissively.

"Your cooperation is appreciated, Mr. Wright." Frida inclines her head toward him, and he smiles, obviously pleased to be praised. "We apologize for pulling you away from your family today, Ezra. We all mourn the death of such a kind and powerful woman."

"Thank you. She'll be missed."

"Can you tell me what you've felt since you've arrived?" Frida asks.

"I'll be honest. I've been distracted for the past couple of days with the funeral. But on the way here, I saw a family of spirits. I was confused as to why they were wandering on the side of the road, especially when my companion, who is a vampire, could see them as well." I continued to ignore Waylon as if I haven't been aware of her every move since she took her seat across from me. "Confused, I stopped to speak with them. They informed me that the light flickered out."

"H-How is that p-possible?" Thomas sputters.

"I wasn't sure, so I called an older spirit to me. She informed me that hallowed ground was the only place safe for the erratic change in the atmosphere. That they could smell the huntsmen on the wind."

"And you believe some old bag of bones?" Thomas asks, exasperated.

"Unlike people, most dead have no reason to lie." I lift my head to meet his gaze, refusing to back down. He looks away, and I smirk. Sometimes it's good to flex a little muscle.

"Could you do that again?" Lazarus' voice slices through the tension like a razor-sharp machete.

"Call her in particular?" I shake my head. "Not without a name. If I went back to about the same spot as before, I could try."

"No. Call on the dead and let them speak for all of us."

"You want a full manifestation?" I whistle. "It'll take some supplies, but I'm up to it if that's what's necessary." Manifesting a person to think independently and appear in the flesh ... well, flesh is a misleading word. "The sacrifice used to call them to me will determine how they come back. I don't do human sacrifice, so they'll never be picture-perfect, but I can make them passable enough to what they once were, depending on the age."

"Would the blood of a vampire freely given work?"

My eyes widen. They don't go around giving donations. Blood is life and power to them. It's a generous offer that shows how serious he is about peace and protecting this area.

"It's the next best thing. Do you have someone in mind?"

"I wanted to pick a person we could all trust." Lazarus glances at Frida, who sits up straight in her chair.

"My aunt, Ingrid." She exhales. "The entire family is behind the decision because we believe in the work being put in to bring all of our people together. The Night Huntsmen do not discriminate with their killing blades. To them, we are abominations who are only good when dead."

Reaching into my satchel, I began to rummage through the supplies I keep at the ready. "I'll need to pick up a few things before the ritual tonight."

A butt cheek clenching howl echoes around the property. My skin pimples up and my body grows cold. Another howl joins in, and another until the baying makes my eardrums quake.

"What is it?" Waylon whispers.

"You don't hear that?" I ask.

"No." She shakes her head.

I glance around at the others watching me like I'm high on crank.

"I don't think the Night Huntsmen are coming. I think they're already here waiting at the gates."

"What do you hear?" Lazarus asks.

"Hounds."

Lazarus stands from the table, instantly on alert. "Where?"

"All around."

"Why can't we hear them?" Frida asks.

"The barriers are still holding. What I'm experiencing must be in the patchy places where they were able to breakthrough." Standing from my seat, I walk toward the sound. Focused, I study the space for cracks or hidden places. Sometimes spirits like to tuck themselves into hidden spaces in certain locations. I didn't feel anything malignant when I walked in, but that doesn't mean anything. Opening my senses, I sweep the house slowly, registering the energies of the inhabitants. Hiding among the undead would be easy to do.

"Can I walk the space?" I glance over my shoulder, and Lazarus nods.

"You have free reign."

Leaving the main room, I turn right and walk down the hallway, making sure no spirits are blending in with the walls that lead deeper into the cellar where more beer was served. Pausing at the end, I block out the continuous howling and look up at the ceiling.

"Do you see something?" Luke asks.

"No, but people always forget to look up. It's a frequent place for spirits to hide."

"And now ceilings will never be the same," Waylon mumbles.

Continuing into the main foyer, a shadow drifts by. I pause, catching it out of the corner of my eyes. Spinning on my heel, I follow the fading opaque shape. Jogging to keep up, I turn the corner and find myself in a dining room. Pausing by the massive structure, I watch as the spirit hovers by the hanging lighting. Tilting my head up, I wait. The energy shimmers, and a woman in a flowing white gown and creamy café au lait skin appears. Dark brown spiral curls frame an oval-shaped slender face with expressive dark brown eyes and familiar delicate features.

"I don't think you need to worry about bringing Ingrid back."

"You see her now?" Frida asks.

"I think so?" The woman nods. Some ghosts speak out loud, others in my mind, or not at all. I don't make the rules, and I've never been told why. "Yeah, it's her."

Ingrid points. "You want me to find something?" She nods her head. "Can you guide me to it?" She nods again.

The stench of rotten eggs forces me to gag. Coughing, I stumble back as the spirit is engulfed in bright red flames. "The wall is thin now," I croak. Snarling comes from the hallway. The others turn, and I know this time, they can hear it. The ghostly black dogs are surrounded by a smoky fog. The stench of sulfur emanates from them, turning my stomach. Saliva drips from their foaming mouths, and fire flickers in the depths of their eyes.

Their bodies arch. Throwing up my hand, I slam my power down, forcing them to the ground.

"Heel, puppy, puppy." Encircling their necks with power like a leash, I gain even more control.

"How did they get in?"

"They're from the fae realm. The same rules don't apply. If you want to keep them out, you need iron. A lot of iron. These aren't your everyday fae. They've got the backing of powerful rulers behind him." They fight me as I speak, struggling against me.

"These three are just the scouting power. I wouldn't want to test the limits of my abilities if their family decides to show up."

"What do you think we should do?" Frida steps up beside me.

Grab our ankles and kiss our ass good-bye?

75

"We can put down a barrier to keep the dead out. It'll help because their magic is based in death."

"I have iron shavings," a tall, tow-haired woman says.

"I can get it. What do I need to do with it?" Lazarus asks.

"Spread it around the perimeter of the home and the doorways."

The feeling of the dead increased as the other members of the Coalition gather around us.

"We can harness energy from your subjects if they're amenable. Create a … holding pen of sorts until the thin spot that allowed them to enter shifts, and their access is cut off."

"Do what you need to," Frida commands.

Slowly ciphering the source that kept them living and not breathing. Envisioning a cage with bars and energy running through each cylinder, I box the three hounds in before I release them. Barking wildly, they throw themselves at the bars. Maddened by their inability to strike, they work themselves into a frothy fury. If this is just the dogs of the hunt, the thought of their owners terrifies me. They flicker, disappearing as suddenly as they appeared.

"What happened?" Waylon asks.

"I'm not sure. The thin space could have closed, or it could be the iron shavings laid down."

"Still need proof the Night Hunt is coming?" Frida

says sarcastically. "No? Good. We'll meet at my family's burial plot at midnight."

"I'll show them out," a tall man with dark hair and dark eyes volunteers, stepping forward.

"Thank you, Alex." Frida smiles.

Unsure if I'm included in the people seeing out, I hesitate. "I have a few things to ready for tonight. If you have any fae favors, I suggest you call them in."

"Can you stay for that?" Lazarus' request is a surprise.

"Me?" I press a hand to my chest. "Listen, putting me anywhere near politics is like setting up for a train wreck."

"The fae beholden to me is from the Unseelie Court. I think he'll find you quite fascinating," Cortez says.

"Are we talking bait or distraction? I don't mind being used to throw them off, but I've seen enough horror movies to know the brown man rarely makes it out alive, usually through no fault of his own." The darker fae have always been curious about necromancers. A human capable of controlling the dead had more power than they thought *magical humans* should be capable of. They're elitists, but from their point of view, who could blame them? They'd been around since before the dawn of time and would continue to be so long after the time of man passes.

Lazarus chuckles. "Distraction. You're worth more to me alive."

Frida shot him a look that made me swallow a smile. Even a king must answer to his queen.

"At least you're honest."

"Please, don't encourage him," Frida scoffs. "How do we call in the marker?"

"Blood magic." Moving to the mantle, he removes the mirror and delicately bites his wrist. Dripping his blood onto the mirror, he places his forefinger in the dark red substance, and begins to trail it in a counterclockwise motion. The surface shimmers, and the red liquid is absorbed. A swirling purple portal opens. A stunning face with full, pink lips, large, violet eyes framed with impossibly long lashes, high cheekbones, and delicate, perfectly symmetrical features framed with white-blond hair appears.

"Aaah. I've wondered when you would settle my debt." His lips part, revealing blinding white teeth that are a little too pointy. He tilts his head, sending his straight locks tumbling. A pointed ear pokes through the silken curtain. If his voice hadn't been so masculine, I would've guessed he was a she.

"Have I contacted you at an appropriate time, Eitri?"

"Yes, I've been quite bored of late. What do you wish of me?" He leans closer, clearly elated. Fae operate differently. Things we view as life and death are but games to them.

"Can you come through, so we can speak?"

"Ooh, a visit to your realm? Do you welcome me?" His face glows with excitement.

"I do."

"Smart. So very smart. You have my word, vampire."

"Then please, come through." Cortez places the mirror on the mantle and steps back. Black smoke pours through the circle into the center of the room. Swirling, it created the shape of a person. A moment later, Eitri arrives. Dressed in black breeches with stockings of the same color and dripping with jewels, he is a relic from a time long past.

"At your service." Eitri bowed, waving his slender hands. His gold-tipped nails catch the light—as deadly as they are beautiful.

"You're at no one's service." Lazarus' voice is wry.

"How true. You play the game so well." Eitri observes the room. "Aaah. I finally get to meet the queen. You caused quite an uproar with this union."

Frida curtseys. "We're honored to have you as a guest in our home."

"What manners." His gaze lands on me. "And what do we have here?" he purrs. "When did you add a necromancer to your stable?"

"He didn't," I answer for myself. Fae are wild. You can't show fear, or they'll find a way to capitalize on it.

"He speaks. Now I'm even more intrigued." Eitri turns to Lazarus. "Why have you brought me here?"

"We ask for whatever assistance you can give us to defeat the Night Hunters."

"You don't ask for anything simple, do you?" Eitri drawls. He tilts his head. "I'm always up for evening the odds. It makes a game more entertaining. And no offense, but you need all the help you can get. The Night Hunt is a nasty bit of business. It was derived from our Wild Hunt." He taps a long nail against his lips. "There is a weapon. A sword meant to fell them. But it can only be wielded by a child of the dead."

"Are their side effects?" I inquire. The fae items always have strings attached.

"Not if the user is strong enough to wield it," Eitri says elusively. "Spoiler alert. You are." Eitri winks.

My brow furrows, and I lift my shoulder in a one-arm shrug. "Why should I trust you?"

"I am bound by the agreement and debt." Eitri turns to face Lazarus. "I will bring the sword, and I will tell you a long-guarded secret to be used with your own discretion. Will that suffice for the marker?"

"You've been generous. Thank you." Lazarus bows.

"I like your kind, vampire. You've retained the best of the old world." Walking to Lazarus, he leans in and whispers into his ear. His eyes widened as Eitri stepped away. "Until next time." Turning into a swirling cloud of black smoke once more, he returns through the mirror the way he'd come. In his wake, a long, black scabbard rests on the floor.

"Do you think child of the dead refers to all vampires or just necromancers?" I question.

"I'm not sure. So far, he only guaranteed you could touch it." Lazarus gestures toward it.

Kneeling, I can feel the power it gives off. I look up at Lou. "Here goes nothing." Wrapping my hand around the sword, I lift it up. I pull the katana free to reveal a silver, angular sword with etchings in a language I don't know.

"You look like you know what you're doing," Lazarus says.

"Just a bit. My father had a collection." Sheathing the sword, I thank him once more for everything he taught me. Even from beyond the grave, my father continues to save my ass.

"I'm tasking you with caring for it then."

"I'll keep it with me at all times." I give a slight bow. "Until the graveyard tonight."

CHAPTER SIX

I've done this a million times before. It's a fairly routine raising. The corpse is older, not ancient, and I've got vampire blood at my disposal. It should be a walk in the park, except the eyes of my peers watching my every move have me off-kilter. Death magic isn't one you can learn. You have to be born into it, or indoctrinated into it by someone who was. It's less a part of what you can do and more who you are at your very core. It is no coincidence. It's a rare type of magic to have. Too many of us messing with death would upset the balance in a major way.

Allowing muscle memory to kick in, I light the medley of herbs I've mixed in my bowls along with the black and white candles.

People forget life and death is linked. You can't have one without the other. death is linked in life. When I resurrect, I'm looking for a balance. I need them to remember who they were in order to get them to talk. I waft the smoke around the circle of salt, obsidian, and lapis lazuli. The circle gives me plenty of room to maneuver and give Ingrid her own space. It's not an exact science, and I can never predict how they'll come back or how long it'll take them to reboot their brains, so to speak. Ingrid would've been a powerful witch in her time. It's possible she could try to resist me.

Satisfied with the environment I've created inside of the circle, I cut a small opening, and gesture toward Frida and Lazarus. Chanting, I watch as they cut open their palms and allow their blood to drip onto the earth. Blood of her kin, and that of a master vampire should help immensely. Wind whips through the graveyard. The clouds shift, blocking the moonlight. My hairs stand on end as the energy begins to gather. The ground starts to move beneath my feet. I can feel her bones rattling inside of her box in the mausoleum.

"I call you, Ingrid Gaumond. By blood, sacrifice, and magic. Through time and planes. So I will it, so must you answer." The blast of power that accompanies my command shocks me. I'm still learning my new strength. Directing my power into the white building, I find her signature.

"Vini. Vini. Vini." Lightning cracks overhead, illuminating the darkened area. I spot a silhouette on the steps of the building.

"She's here."

Stepping out of the shadows, Ingrid appears in the same white dress. Mist winds its way around her ankles like a cat. Her cheeks are sunken in, and her collarbone stands out sharply. Her eyes are impossibly dark, and her lips are painted red with the blood offering.

"They don't want me to speak with you." Her voice is wind moving through bamboo.

"Who?" I ask.

"The Night Huntsmen." She looks around almost nervously.

What would the dead need to fear? Unsettled, I scan the area around her for signs of something being off.

"This time is different. Their final hunt. And they plan on going out in style."

"What does that mean, Ingrid?" I ask gently.

She licks the blood from her lips, and I tense, ready to respond if she tries to rush me.

"They will run wild until they're put down."

"No. The terms are a twenty-four-hour period," a male voice protests from behind me.

"They have powerful allies. I came to warn you. The huntsmen are no longer working alone."

"Who are they working with?"

"I don't know. They're powerful enough to deal with the fae. They traded." Her brows come together.

"For what?" I prompt.

"I don't know," she cries. Coming back isn't an easy process. I don't want to burn her out.

"It's okay," I say softly.

"All I can share is what I see. I came to help my kin, so she can succeed where we all failed." Her lower lip trembles. Her head moves, and she's looking past me.

"Are we done listening to her ramble on?" Thomas asks snarkily. Grunting, he goes down onto one knee.

"A little respect is required when dealing with a lady," Lazarus says cooly.

"Use your magic against me again, vampire, and see what happens."

"Is that a threat?" Frida asks. Her voice is deadly calm, like a placid ocean just before a hurricane.

"This is between men," Thomas barks.

Frida moves too fast to track. I jump, and Thomas scrambles back to avoid her, toppling onto his ass. *How can a mere witch move like that?* I scan her with my magic once more, and she continues to read as a witch. If she's gained speed from Lazarus, what has he gained from her? *Power couple has a whole new meaning with these two.*

"You want to repeat that?" Frida asks, staring down at him.

"Abomination." Thomas spits the words like a curse.

"Evolution," Lazarus' tone is so frosty is could freeze lava.

"Progress," Ingrid replies shakily, redirecting our attention. "They keep us separated with our guns aimed at one another for selfish, fear-based reasons. Over here, things are suddenly so much clearer."

"I think we'll take your word on it for now, my dear," Luke says.

"How can we defeat the Night Huntsmen?" I ask.

"Iron, and a concentrated group effort. It's vital—" Her body stiffens, and she glances over her shoulder. The temperature plummets. My breath billows out in a white cloud. I seal the circle I opened to allow for the blood donation.

"He's coming." Her shrill voice is chilling.

"Who?"

A dark gloved hand wraps around her mouth. Her eyes widen, and her body is yanked back into the door frame. The pull on her connection feels like a T-rex ready for a game of tug-o-war. Planting my feet, I wrap my connection with Ingrid tight and yank back. A wizened face appears behind her. Green skin, sunken features, and dark eyes full of rage and hate center on me. His lips peel back to reveal jagged teeth, and he spews darkness. Throwing up a shield, I know instinctively I don't want to be touched by it in any way.

As the evil engulfs Ingrid and tries to travel to me via our connection, I cut the cord linking us. Rooted between worlds, the huntsmen have found a way to reach us. As they disappear into the darkness, I quickly rescind my invitation to her. Kneeling inside of the circle, I make sure he's actually gone.

"How was that possible?" Frida asks.

"He's got powerful friends. Death magic is not easily wielded. I don't believe he's doing these things under his own power."

"The Unseelie?" someone guesses.

"Why? They've gotten what they needed from them. Their bodies have been used up. For them, the huntsmen have served their purpose." Lazarus shakes his head.

"But we know there's a third party invested in this now," Frida adds.

"The question is what could they hope to gain?" Luke's furrowed brow, adds years to his age.

Lazarus shrugs. "With all of us gone, the entire territory. Power is an incredible motivator."

"The question is, whose enemy are we dealing with?" Frida shakes her head.

"I think the correct answer to that question is ours. The animosity and pettiness will have to be set aside for us to survive this and come out on top. It's us or them. There's no room for separation any longer." He stares everyone down, daring them to disagree.

A murmur of agreement is reached.

"Is she okay, Ez?" Frida asks me softly.

"I don't know. There's not much that can truly harm the dead." I think of the book that's thrown me into this situation. "I can find out for you." It's time for me to spend more time with the *Book of the Dead*.

"You don't have to take your master's orders so literally," I say as I glance over my shoulder and find Waylon a few steps away.

"Dude. How are you not taking things more seriously?" Her exasperated tone is nails across a chalkboard.

"I am. What I don't see is how you being underfoot is helpful."

"He told me to stay close."

"Ahhh." I make a buzzer sound. "All he asked was us to work together. We can do that without breathing down each other's necks."

"Bitter isn't a good look on you, E," she whispers.

"Funny, since you were the one who picked out this outfit for me. And it's Ez to you." The nickname singed me like fire now.

"We need to clear the air."

As we reached the front door, I shut her down. "Let's not and say we did."

"This isn't helping anyone."

I grind my teeth as I unlock the door and push it open. The house is empty. *Thank God for small miracles.* Stepping inside, I close the door behind her and lock it. Hanging my jacket on the peg beside the door, I pause.

She throws her hands up and lets them drop, slapping the sides of her thighs.

"No. It's not helping you. You have no clue what it does or doesn't do for me. That was always your problem, though, wasn't it? You never saw the big picture or thought about the damage your choices could do. Instead, it was all about you."

"I was trying to survive in a world I didn't fully understand. You know my story."

I peer down at her, refusing to give an inch. Our entire relationship I folded to her like a lawn chair. "And you knew mine. What did you think it would to me, Waylon?"

She cringes. "I don't know." Her head drops. "I wasn't thinking about that. I saw this opportunity to have the one thing I've longed for since I was changed, and I ... went for it."

"Exactly. 'Cause you didn't care half as much about me as I did you."

"That's not fair."

"You know what I've learned? Life's not fair. All we can do is deal with what it gives us and try to stay sane. The general rule of thumb, if it's not hurting you, you don't get to judge what method others choose to live this life."

"It does. Seeing you look at me with hate and disgust is like a knife to the gut."

Her soft admission throws me off. *Are we finally being honest and real?*

"We are all fucked up by the things that happened to us and trying to move forward, Waylon. You don't get to use that excuse as an explanation for your fucked-up behavior."

"Imagine being changed at sixteen into a creature you thought was a myth, Ez. I went to a party like most teenagers my age. I didn't get drunk or do drugs. I drank one beer and found myself at the wrong place with the wrong person. He ripped my throat out, left me for dead in the back yard, and changed life as I knew it. I nearly burned to death sitting out there in the sun. I had to hide in their shed until nightfall, with my stomach eating itself from the inside out." Her shoulders shake.

I want her to stop talking, but I can't bring myself to say the words. She never went into detail about the change. It'd been too fresh.

"I think I knew. I hadn't suddenly developed a disease that made me allergic to sunlight, and I had a chunk taken out of my neck. My new navy-blue dress with geometric shapes was covered in blood, and my pink jellies were a dusty light red. I felt like my stomach was eating itself from the inside out, and my throat was so dry. I had never known thirst and hunger like this. It was overwhelming. As I waited for the sun to set, I became delirious. I started to relive the attack and pick up on things, like the way his eyes flashed red, and how his sharp teeth flashed white a second before he struck. How I hadn't even tried to fight."

The thrall. Imagining her so vulnerable and confused hurt my heart. She grips the bottom of her black Smoky the Bear T-shirt in her fisted hands.

"One look and I was suddenly frozen in my body. I couldn't understand why I wouldn't fight." Her voice cracks. "The sunset and I slipped from the shed, desperate to see my family. I knew once I told my parents they'd make everything okay again. I'd see a doctor or a specialist." She sighed. "When I got there, I knew I was in deep shit. My parents had gone out to look for me, and my baby brother, Dalton, was the only one left home, in case I decided to show up. He almost knocked me over. He hugged me so hard. They were all terrified I'd been kidnapped or killed. I was a good girl. I didn't stay out all night with no word." She shakes her head, lost in her memories. "I never would've done that to my parents. I was so relieved to be home. I forgot about everything else. I went upstairs, showered, and came down to find something to eat. I heated up the lasagna while my stomach growled. The second I took my first bite, I knew it was a mistake. I gagged, and purged it in the sink immediately. My brother ran in to check on me, and that's when I noticed his heartbeat."

No. My heart ached for her.

"Next, I noticed how good he smelled. Before I could think about it, I was moving. My teeth sank into his skin, and he screamed out. His blood hit my taste buds and I was lost." Tears rolled down her cheeks. "He cried out, 'Stop, please! Why? Why?' and somehow it reached me. I released him and stumbled back. He slumped to the ground. His heartbeat was thready and weak. God. I almost killed him. This little kid who'd been my shadow. Whose diapers I'd changed. I knew then I had to leave because I no longer belonged."

"So, you left?" I ask softly.

"And never came back because I'd rather die than kill someone I loved. I spent the years learning to hunt on my own, staying to myself, and avoiding extended time with humans until I gained more control. And then ... until you. I never had one on one that way."

"What do you mean until me, Waylon?"

"I never wanted to spend that much time with humans. You were the temptation I knew I should resist, but didn't. I thought I was ready."

"Are you saying now you weren't?"

"Emotionally, I was. Maturity wise in vampire years with no training?" She shook her head. "But I wanted to be."

"Why wouldn't you tell me this then?"

"Pride? Shame? Stupidity that only comes with youth?"

Inhaling through my nose, I peer up at the ceiling. "What is this supposed to change?"

"I needed you to know."

"And now what do I do?" The young boy from the past is speaking for me as I'm taken back to the moment that would shape my life irrevocably. "When my parents found out about you, they hit the roof. My mother made my life a living hell for a year and a half, but to me, it was worth it to have you. They gave me an ultimatum, do you remember? Break up with you or move out. What did I do, Waylon?" I hold my hand up to my ear and wait.

"You got your own place."

"That's right. It was a subpar studio, but it was mine. Which meant I got to live by my own rules. Leaving you never even entered my mind."

"What good would our relationship be if I ripped

out your throat? Do you know what induced blood lust? Strong emotions, lust, sex. Guess what trifecta we had going on constantly?"

Her words silence me momentarily. "What are you saying?"

"I started losing time and seeing visions. I wasn't ready to handle us in a safe way. Too much over too much time and shitty coping skills. I shorted out. I didn't want to tell you or scare you. Then I met them, and they seemed to have the keys to living life as a vampire. When they presented themselves to me, they were so nice. A group of people looking to add new members to a misfit band of vampires."

"That's every bad guy's M.O., Waylon."

"I know that now. They got into my head, started talking about how we were meant to be entangled. I didn't buy into that until they began telling me horror stories about human and vampire pairings that all ended in death and insanity."

"Why wouldn't you tell me this?"

She stares at the ground. "You gave up everything for me, and I couldn't hack it."

"So, you humiliate me instead? Denied being with me in front of people you hardly knew and turned your back on the life we were building?"

"Yes, damn it. 'Cause it was better than me wailing over your corpse," she snaps. Her eyes glow amber.

I close my eyes. "I can't do this with you now, Waylon."

"I know. It's why I didn't say anything. Then you kept judging me without the full picture. I know I made bad decisions. But back then, I had no one to turn to and it was the best of the worst. I was with that group long enough to learn a few things, and then I ran into Frida and … things progressed from there."

"You never even tried to contact me."

"I didn't have the right. Doesn't mean I didn't keep tabs mind you."

Disconcerted by her reveal, I run a hand through my hair and sigh. "All right. Later, we'll talk. Right now, I have a ghost to find. We can be civil, right?"

"That's all I wanted to be, Ez."

"Good. That's … good." I scoop my melting brain back into its jar and walk toward the basement. Pausing, I hold out my hand. "Wait here. I'll bring the book up, okay?"

"Okay."

After days of strained silence and resentment, we've reached an accord. I've never been so grateful to have an issue to focus on. Taking the stairs two at a time, I hurry to the book's hidey-hole. Linked to my blood and magic, it's impossible for anyone else to find, let alone remove the book.

Hefting the bound book, I retrace my steps. I plop

down on the couch, open it, and begin to sift through the pages.

"What exactly are you looking for?" Waylon asks.

"I'm not sure yet." A section called 'names of the dead' catches my eye.

"Since when do you read hieroglyphics?"

"What?"

She gestured toward the page.

"That's how it looks to you?"

"Yeah. You see it differently?"

"It's English for me."

"Clever."

"The book has a mind of its own, that's for sure." Turning to the chapter, my jaw drops. It's like a computer screen with names constantly moving in and out of focus. Locations are tagged on behind them. "Wow."

"What?"

"I think I just found ghost GPS." The names didn't seem to have a particular rhyme or reason. *Maybe if I ask for her. Show me Ingrid Gaumond, please.* The names swirl together, creating a whirlpool of letters. Ingrid Gaumond. St Mary Cemetery. Relieved, I pull the phone out of my satchel and text Lou.

She's back at rest where she belongs.

My phone chimes a second later. **Thank God.**

"Now what?"

"Now we go see an old friend about a ghost. You might want to skip this part, though."

"Aim?"

I nod. "Yeah. You aren't her favorite person."

Waylon frowns, her brow furrowing. "That's like saying the pope is just a little Catholic, Ez."

"You don't have to go." I shrug.

"You know damn well I do." She growls. "Come on, let's get this over with. We need to swing by my house so I can change and get more clothing."

"Inviting yourself over for a slumber party?" I ask sarcastically as I shrug on a long trench coat; I've taken the lining out and sewn a pocket to conceal the sword.

"Doing my job."

"Hmm," I grunt. It's going to be an interesting night.

CHAPTER SEVEN

W hat is this place? I've never noticed it before," Waylon says as we pull into the semi-crowded parking place in front of the old wooden building that was clearly a renovated church. A blue neon sign spells out Neco.

"You weren't meant to. This is for necromancers. It caters to a small group. We're loyal and eager to swap stories and information if properly motivated."

Waylon stills in the passenger seat. "You expect me to walk into a bar full of witches who specialize in controlling the dead?"

"Eh, it's more of a gaming hall."

"That's what you got out my sentence?" she asks incredulously.

"You're with me. I'm not going to let anything hurt you. That hasn't changed."

Our eyes meet, and she exhales. "I'm placing my life in your hands." Her fingers grip the seatbelt strapped across her tight.

"I did suggest you stay home." I say blandly.

"Really!" She growls.

I snicker. "Where's the lie in that statement?" I grow serious. "Consider my track record. Have I ever let you down when you needed me?"

"No," she says softly.

"There you go. Now, let's get a move on. Night is burning, and you have a sunrise curfew." I unbuckle my seatbelt and move from the car.

"You were a lot more gracious in my memory." She says loud enough for me to hear.

"Time changes all things," I croon, and open her door from her out of habit

"I can be in daylight, you know?" She rises from the car.

"Yes, but it runs down your reserves." I lean over the door peering down at her. "I know how much it takes to maintain that particular spell, and you're without official affiliation. I assume it's why you're pledging for the Coalition?" The wind ruffles my straight thick dark hair. I catch a glimpse of myself in the sideview mirror and scowl at the longish nose I'd inherited from my mother. Thick eyebrows, downturned medium brown eyes, and thin lips are the most prominent features handed down from my father.

"Among other reasons." Being a part of a powerful group has its perks; protection and a power upgrade are included in the joining package. It was also the reason they had trail periods. Acceptance into their fold wasn't given lightly. She moves past me, and I shut the door. "How long have you been putting in your bid for a spot?"

"About a year. I'm nearing decision time. This is going to make or break." She falls into step beside me.

"Answer a question honestly. For me," I ask despite my better judgment.

"Okay?" Turning her head, she meets my gaze and we slow our walk.

"Did you volunteer for this, or did they send you?"

"Ez ..."

"You've already answered me." I wave her off. I'm still trying to digest the things she revealed earlier. I'm looking forward to some time in Neco's environment among friends and others like me. Here I'm among my own people in more ways than one. Stepping inside, I extend a portion of my power to surround Waylon. Heads turn from the bar.

"She's with me." I stand tall, staring them all down.

It's not unheard of for vampires and necromancers to run in the same circle, but it's rare. The talking resumes, and a squeal threatens to blow my eardrum.

"E!"

Spinning, I turn and open my arms to accept the bundle of energy swathed in a pastel blue dress with a white collar that reminds me of Alice in Wonderland.

"A." I hug her tight to my chest and inhale her sweet scent. "I've missed you."

"With everything going on, I didn't expect to see you before you hauled ass out of this town."

"Yeah, well, me either. I had an unexpected change of plans." I lower her to the ground. "Things aren't what they seem."

"What?" She pulls back, and her nose crinkles. She peers beside me, and her entire body goes stiff as a board. "I know I'm not seeing what I think I'm seeing." Her eyes narrow into slits. The energy in the room spikes.

"Aminthe." Waylon stands her ground.

"Ezra?"

"She's here with me on Lazarus' orders."

"Finally realized you were in with a pit of vipers? Too little too late. I will tolerate your presence in my establishment for now. But don't make the mistake of believing you're welcome in any way."

"I wouldn't dream of it."

"You have explaining to do." Aim crosses her arms and turns, stalking toward the back room where she all but lived most days.

Entering her pastel palace, I take a seat on the tufted pink pull-out couch with shiny square gems sewn in. Waylon chooses to stand instead, leaning against the wall beside me.

Aim sinks into the chair I playfully refer to as her pink throne. The pastel pink wing-back is also bejeweled and fitting of a queen with its whimsical curved edges. Crossing her ankles, she leans back. "Start talking, E."

"I was on my way back out of town when I was stopped by Waylon. I never would've given her the time of day, but she had an official message from Cortez."

"Okay, so I won't have to strangle you. Why are you still together?"

"Because he wants us to work together. I won't stand here and be talked about as if I don't exist."

Aim pins her with eyes that glow amber. "I'll let you know when I'm ready to listen to your voice."

"I am not a dog." Waylon's fangs elongate, and she hisses.

"Please, give me a reason, vampire. You broke my best friend's heart. I've been itching to pay you back in pain."

"A, you're the dopest best friend a guy could have, but right now isn't the time or place. We've got huge problems. I'm sure I'm not the only one who noticed the dead are behaving oddly, and there all kinds of patchy spots where things that shouldn't be are slipping through into our plane."

Sitting up straighter in her chair, she leans forward. "There's been a lot of talk about the topic in the gaming rooms recently. You know how we run our mouths during campaigns."

"I do."

"Gaming room?" Waylon adds.

Aminthe scowls. "Neco has a lively gaming community. We have back rooms dedicated to it."

"That's amazing."

"You have to be one of us to get in or know someone willing to vouch for you and extend some of their essence."

"What?"

"Magical energy. You can't feel him?" Aim scoffs.

She turns to me, surprised. "I thought it was linked to this place." Placing a hand over her heart, she closes her eyes.

"Why would you think that?" Aim asks.

"Because if I knew coming here would make me feel like this, I'd be a regular, too."

"Feel like what?" I ask cautiously.

"Nope." She shakes her head, popping the p.

Since I've given up trying to understand women when they're being cryptic, for mental health reasons, I let the subject matter drop.

"Why is Cortez interested in ghost matters?" Aim asks.

"Because they're all related to the Night Hunt."

The blood rushes from her face, and her fingers dig into the arms of the couch. "Please tell me I heard you wrong."

"I wish I could."

"Are they sure?"

"I actually did a resurrection to speak with a ghost who'd come to warn us earlier. It's one hundred percent official. The huntsmen are on their way back quick, fast, and in a hurry."

Her mouth presses into a flatline. "Shit."

"Exactly. I had my session interrupted by a Night Huntsman."

"What? Tell me everything, and don't leave out any details."

Making myself comfortable on the couch, I launch into the retelling of the event still fresh in my mind.

"How is that possible? They exist in the realm of fae. Crossing over like this shouldn't be possible in theory."

"She said they have powerful allies now and that the old rules no longer apply."

"Who, short of a neco, could help them accomplish that, E? This is bad."

"I've had the same thoughts, but I keep coming up blank. We're practically a law unto ourselves, who among us would willingly deal with the creatures responsible for the death of so many of our kind?"

"A person who feels disassociated from other witches. It's no secret you guys are on the fringes. Is it so inconceivable someone would want to give them a taste of their own medicine?" Waylon shrugs.

I fight down the annoyance that rises as she speaks on issues I once shared with her. "The Night huntsmen don't discriminate. It means the death of all who crossed their path," I say.

"When you aren't thinking straight, you can't see the big picture," Waylon states.

Aim sneers. "You'd know all about that. Wouldn't you?"

"Yeah, I would. Which is why you should listen to me. I'm sure when he or she was approached, the offer was prettied up and pitched in the most appealing manner possible. Whatever that person lacked, they made it seem as if they had all the answers to the problems. It's how they indoctrinate you."

"Suddenly, you're a cult specialist?"

"The Lovecraft Court didn't want a family. They

wanted blind followers. Strict rules, strange rituals, and lack of freedom that slowly creep into your daily routine until you're imprisoned. Isolated from everyone you know, you're afraid that there's really no reason to leave, and that they will never let you be free."

"And how, pray tell, did you waltz away without so much as a scratch?"

"Who says I have? I'm still not sure I escaped them, and the escape was anything but easy." She shuddered, rubbing her arms. "You can judge me for my past actions, but you don't get to speak on things you can't possibly understand."

"We should get out there and gather information. Maybe we can piece together more clues." I quickly insert myself in the silence between them before either can pick back up with the attitude. It won't help us get any closer to solving things, and it could be bad for their health. A has never been one to back down, and Waylon is a wild card. I can't pretend to know how she'd respond.

"I doubt they'll talk with her here," Aim says.

"They will when they hear Waylon came in for a game. That she's thinking of coming back onto the scene," I say.

"Bitch," Aim grumbles. "Fine. Go start up a few games, let the alcohol and competition loosen tongues, and I'll mingle and see what I can turn up. We'll meet back here before Cinderella needs to leave to avoid her carriage turning back into a pumpkin. It's a shame they don't make a better SPF for your little sun problem."

"Or did they?" Waylon widens her eyes, mocking her.

"Okay, we're going to pick up a game. We'll see you soon." I wrap my arm around Waylon's waist and quickly usher her out of the back room.

"Why did you do that? I could handle her."

"Uh-huh. I figured avoiding the whole messy business was the smarter route. Look alive. You're about to delve back into the world of gaming. How long has it been since you even rolled?"

She grimaced. "Longer than I care to admit."

"This should be interesting then."

"Are you saying you doubt my playing abilities?" Her calm tone doesn't fool me. She's fired up.

"I don't know where your skill level is currently, Waylon. I do know these are avid players who are constantly improving."

Her nostrils flare. "We'll see."

We enter one of the rooms in the back set up for gaming, and she hums her approval. With the round table, comfy chairs, snack bar, and waitress weaving in and out it's nerd heaven.

"It's like Vegas for nerds," she marvels.

The whispers begin. A brown-skinned boy with a killer afro and easy toothpaste commercial white grin saunters up to us. "Are you Waylon?"

"You remember me?" she asks.

"Oh yeah. You were a legend. I think we were all sorry to see you go. Are you coming back?"

She glances at me. "Dipping my toe into the water and seeing how it feels."

"I can understand that. I'm Xander." He holds out his hand, and she shakes it, playing nice. "And don't think I didn't recognize you, Ezra. You're legendary in more than just gaming circles."

"I don't know if I'm wary or proud of that."

"Proud, definitely." Xander cheeses like a fool. Dimples appear in his cheek. His expressions are a little too practiced and polished. I can tell he's used to charming his way through life. He holds out his hand.

I shake, taking the time to read him. He's not nearly as harmless as he portrays himself to be. The power running through him is potent. I incline my head in a show of respect.

"Do you think it'd be possible for us to pick up a game?" I ask.

"For you two? I think the problem will happen when you're ready to stop playing for the night. Come on, I'll show you around. It's probably changed since you last visited. Aminthe is great with keeping things up to date and fresh."

I take in the round tables covered in green felt. Each

space has a cup holder built in. As usual, she remained at the forefront with her concepts, making changes that provided a better experience in Neco. I admire her business savvy. People took one look at her cheerful pastel aesthetic and wrote her off. It was a mistake.

The buzz in the room grows louder as eyes focus on us. It's not too long before we're seated at a table and beginning a new game. It's been a long time since I played with this many people surrounding me. The excitement flowing inside of me has me vibrating on a higher level. *I've missed this.* As I bring my sorcerer to life, I keep my ears open to the conversations going on around me. They're all a little baffled and uneasy about the death energy ramping up in this area. Ghost activity is at an all-time high, and they've been seeing ancestors who usually stay on their plane.

I roll the dice and land a two. Listening to the master explain my fate, I focus in on the conversation happening to my right.

"I've seen a lot of ghosts, but something about this one was off. I couldn't put my finger on it, though."

"I rest and heal from my battle with the Orc," I say.

The master moves on to the next player.

"Did I hear you say you saw something unusual? We saw a displaced family of ghosts on the side of the road earlier. I had to call another ghost to guide them home."

The blonde turns to me. "Did they say why?"

"They said the light disappeared on them."

Whispers spring up like hissing snakes around the table.

"What would cause that?" a voice from across the table inquires.

"A serious disturbance. I'm not sure if …" the blonde hesitates, casting a look at Waylon, "new couplings have contributed to the imbalance, but I know they've addressed it boldly and tried to combat it in their own ways. I had my doubts when things first started to change, but as they say, actions speak louder than words." The blonde shrugs.

"Things have changed more than I ever thought possible," I mumble.

"Some say for the better," the blonde adds.

"Do you remember where the odd experience occurred?"

"Yeah, I do. If you ask around, I think you could get a pretty good start to your map."

I nod. "Do you think the others would be as open to talk about it?" I try to gauge the atmosphere.

"Yeah, it's been a hot topic for the past few months, honestly. Because the energy has been shifting drastically for some time."

"What's the general school of thought about why this is happening?" I keep my eyes on the game happening.

"We've always had a surplus of energies here. From the Native Americans who practice, to the wronged slaves who brought their magic and beliefs as well as their animosity. Many wrongs have been committed here, and that negative energy adds up. It's possible someone or something decided to take advantage of that." The blonde shrugs.

"By siphoning the energy for their own purposes. What would be the payoff?" I ask.

"Chaos? Something we couldn't possibly guess."

"Hmmm." I worry the card between my fingers and let the topic of conversation shift. Another game lands me on the opposite side of the room with a group of new faces playing Dead of Winter. The Zombie apocalypse-based game is made more exciting when it's played with magic. Cole Winters is a new character added with the expansion. The pharmacist and the new graveyard location are intriguing. The game goes for about thirty minutes before the unusual spiritual activity is brought up.

It feels good to be back in my element surrounded by people just like me. Magical beings tend to gravitate toward certain places of power. It's one of the many reasons why there are so many necromancers in the area, which is rare. *Maybe that contributed to the Night Hunt coming about again.*

"I'm telling you, all of this is a sign of something bigger. I've heard rumors about the Night Hunt."

I zero in on the brunet male seated diagonally from me. "The Night Hunt?" I question.

He nods. "People think the Night Huntsmen are waking once more from their slumber. We defeated them by coming together, and that cooperation has been forgotten. As much as people are trying to pull us together now, the damage has been done."

"It's been ages since the last Night Hunt," a male across from him protests.

"Exactly why it'd be past due. These thin places popping up left and right are a sign of them trying to gain entrance to our world."

"Has anyone looked into the thin spots?" I question.

The brunet shakes his head. "Not that I know of."

"Seems like someone should." I shrug.

"Are you nominating yourself?" a blonde asks.

"Yeah. I think I am." I nod. "I believe trying to create a map of sorts to see if there's a nexus would be a good place to start." I keep my voice casual.

An older man with silver threaded through his dark hair clears his throat. "Grab a pen and paper. I have a number of locations for you. If I were a younger man or more powerful, I'd have investigated. But the magic coming from these places makes the hair on the back of my neck stand straight up. It's not for the faint of heart." He has an earthy, grounded feeling. His magic would surely be the same. While he might not be the strongest necro-mancer, his magic would come from a pure, honest place which would make his success rates higher. Might doesn't always make right in the world of magic.

The haunted look in his dark gaze is a warning sign I don't intend to ignore.

"What happened?"

"I thought I'd nose around, see what I could find out." His eyes glaze over, and I know he's back at the site. "The entire area felt tainted. Like the ground had gone bad. The plants surrounding it were all drained. Not just dead, shriveled up as if the life had been drained from them. I'm not ashamed to admit I'm not the hero type. I was only investigating because this particular place was a lit-tle too close to the community I live in. We take care of our own."

I nod in understanding.

"My head was screaming for me to turn around, but my body didn't obey. I had to get closer."

Gut churning, I sit up straighter. "Are you saying something took over?"

"It was like listening to a siren's song. I had to get closer. To see for myself." His voice grew reedy. "I found myself at the base of the biggest Cypress tree I'd ever seen. It sat partially in the water and partially on land. Its limbs were gnarled and twisted. The ridged stump had a giant split in it. I crouched down to look inside." He shuddered. "All I saw was darkness. The energy had its tender hooks embedded deep in me, and I knew I was going to reach inside and get myself killed like the first person to die in a horror movie. Then a snake slithered in front of me, breaking the hold. If it wasn't for my animal guide …" He shook his head. "I stood and hauled ass right outta there. I haven't told anyone else 'bout that experience until now."

"Could you find this tree again?"

"I won't go back there, but I can tell you how to get to it. I put a 'notice me not' ward up to try to keep people from stumbling on it." He dropped his head, clearly ashamed. "It's all I could do."

"Knowing our limits is a necessary survival skill," I assure him.

He nods, and we let the game take the edge off the information he's spilled. This tree sounds like a portal. The question is where does it lead and who controls it? I need to prepare properly. The last thing I want on my grave is death by tree.

Pulling onto the main road, the tires eat up the miles between Neco and the Coalition's home like a ravenous animal. We have an hour until sunrise.

"What did you find out? I have a magically charged tree to inspect."

"The Lovecraft Court is on a new recruiting mission. They've been seen slinking around in the shadows and propositioning baby vampires. They make people uneasy." She scowls.

"You think it's more than that?"

"It always is with them. I don't know why they'd have to be in this territory. It's not their home base. They wanted this to get back to me. To let me know I'm not forgotten or out of their reach. Until I'm pledged into the Cortez Court, I'm technically a free agent. They can hurt me and get away with it."

"Do you think they want to?"

"Yes. You don't just leave them. That was the whole point."

"Then how did you walk away?" I press for more information.

"I didn't. I fought my way out, and I barely made it."

I turn to glance at her, stunned. "Fought?"

"Tooth and nail. I crawled out of there a broken, bloody mess."

"And your clan?"

"Badly injured and furious. I risked my own life to cast the spell that took them out. I hid for a long time afterward, licking my wounds and coming up with a plan."

"And you decided to turn to another clan?" I ask in disbelief.

"No. I got a job and a small apartment. Then fate placed me and Frida in the same place. Eventually, we became friends, and it went from there." The fact that her life hasn't been a bed of roses since she walked into the sunset with the Lovecraft Court pleases me more than it should. I'd never wish the kind of pain she experienced on anyone, but the petty bastard that lives inside of me is glad she had tough lessons to learn. If her life had been rainbows and sunshine, it would a been a kick in the crotch.

"How do you plan on dealing with this?"

"I need to talk to Lazurus," she says softly.

"You think?"

"Could you take a chill pill, and stop being such a barf bag? This is hard enough to deal with without you acting so heinous."

"If you're seeking sympathy, I'd suggest you look elsewhere. The choices you made affected us both. I would say I never wished you ill, but I'd be a liar. I don't take pleasure in your pain. But it doesn't move me. You broke us, Waylon. I'm not going to pretend otherwise. The only thing we agreed to was civility. I think I'm upholding my end of the bargain well. We aren't kids anymore. Our actions had consequences." *Forgetting what she did, regardless of the reasoning, would only lead to disappointment and pain. Been there, done that, and got the T-shirt and the mug.*

I squash the seeds of guilt trying to take root. Dickishness is allowed for self-preservation.

CHAPTER EIGHT

"You owe me for this," Aim says as we carefully pick your way down the trail, headed deeper into the woods.

"Anything you want."

"You to stick around for a while. It's not the same without you."

"You know better than most why I stay away," I say with a sigh.

"I do. But it feels like bullcrap that you have to keep away. This is your home." She trails her fingers over the moss-covered tree. I'd forgotten how green my town could be in the wild. Life in the city had distances me from the beauty of the outdoors.

"I'm not sure it ever was really. I miss you, and some of the food and familiar spots, but that's it. Ain't much to show for eighteen years of living." The wind whistles through the trees, stirring my hair and tickling my neck.

"Things are different now, though, Ez." She kicks at the bright green vegetation lining the first path.

I sneer. "Why? Because I have more power?" I tip my head back to peer up at the massive pine trees towering above us.

"Yes, and with that more responsibility. Your aunt helped people. They'll be looking toward you to fill the space her passing left."

"Sorry for them."

"Ez!"

"I refuse to get pulled back into family business. Ari was always the golden child. Let him step up." I inhale, breathing in the comforting scent of damp earth.

"He can't, and you know it."

"Not my problem."

"The universe has a way of making things our problem when we're stubborn."

I stop abruptly, and she stumbles to avoid running into the back of me.

"What the hell?"

"You obviously have something you want to say to me. We've never been the type to bite our tongue, so let's clear the air before we move forward."

She exhales. "You know I miss having you a drive away, but I've always respected your reasons for leaving and never looking back. Cutting toxic relationships, be they romantic or familial, is a must to be happy and stay sane." She pauses. "You've been gone for three years, and things have changed drastically. Our town needs help."

"Why does that fall back on me?"

"Because there aren't that many necromancers. It's clear from the breaks in our boundaries, things have become unbalanced. Defeating the huntsmen isn't going to be enough. It'll take time and energy to repair the damage that's put us in the precarious position."

"And I'm supposed to do what, Aim?"

"Help build the type of town we always wanted to see."

Clicking my tongue, I shake my head. "We tried that."

"When we were younger and nameless. They have to listen to you now, Ez. Don't you see? You have the power to bring real change to this archaic system." Her eyes plead with me, begging me to do the one thing that could kill my soul.

"I wish I could be the person you think I am."

"Don't reject it outright, Ez. At least think on it."

I tilt my head back and stare up at the canopy of trees leaning toward the sun until they appear to be bowing to one another like dancers about to perform a dance.

Clenching my teeth, I push past my emotional response to hear the truth in her words. The town is in a bad way. Just traveling through it, I can feel how fragmented it's become. Cracks are letting in dangerous things and weakening the balance that kept things in check.

"How long has tension been this high?" I ask.

She hums. "A couple of years."

"Why didn't you say anything?" I ask, stunned.

"Because you weren't ready to hear it. I respected your need to start a new life away from here. You needed to heal back then. There was nothing you could do."

Am I going to let my town perish because I'm butt hurt over poor treatment? It's a question I'm not able to answer. I bow my head. "I'll think about it."

She holds up her hands. "That's all anyone can ask."

"Are we good now?"

"We were always good, Ez. This was just me getting things off my chest."

"I feel you." I crane my neck to study the tall, moss-covered trees that rise up into the heavens, creating a wall of green around us. Any other day I'd enjoy a trek through the forest with my best friend. Today, the misty air that gave everything an ethereal appearance felt sinister. We'd been traveling for just over an hour and my chest was growing tight as my Spidey senses started to tingle. Rolling my shoulders, I glanced at the upcoming fork in the path. I could almost see the difference in lighting as I peered at the right side and back to the left. My instincts told me to steer clear of whatever lay along the pathway on the left.

"There's something wrong here," Aim whispered.

"You feel it, too?" I tilt my head to the side and angle my body to face the source of my unease.

Nodding her head, she cringes. "We're surrounded by life, yet all I can focus on is the creeping sense of death radiating from that direction." She nods her head toward the left path and frowns. Her brows furrow. "It more than the death of a person."

"There's a lack of life. An emptiness that shouldn't be there," I mumble, feeling like I'm being pulled toward a black hole.

"Are we prepared for this?" she whispers.

"We have to be. I don't trust anyone else with the information, or to have my back, Aim. It's always been us against the world. Why would the apocalypse be any different?" I ask flippantly.

She smirks. "Truth." She holds up her fist, and I bump it with my own. "Let's do this."

Gripping the strap of my satchel, I take the lead and ignore the flesh crawling warnings as I move toward the darkness.

"It's not even trying to hide," she whispers.

"What do you mean?"

"The other night you said they mentioned they were taken by surprise. Anyone with even a drop of magic or working intuition would steer clear."

"Maybe it's been well fed?" I suggest.

"Or it's rolling out the welcoming mat for us," she counters.

"Neither theory is reassuring." Her words hit me like a brick. "You think it's cognizant?"

"And old. Possibly corrupted. There are so many things that lie dormant in the ground beneath us. Things perhaps we've forgotten about, or come to think of as legend. To the rest of the world, necromancers don't exist. So, how can we truly discredit anything?"

A chill races down my spine. Thoughts of the dark legends of the forests fill my head. Dark elves with sharp claws and charcoal skin consort with wendigos as they watch us from behind the trees in my mind. The hair on my body rises, and I have to force my feet to keep moving. The trees grow closer together, blotting out the sun. The mist thickens, and the sound of a waterfall emerges.

"Do you remember there being a waterfall here?" I ask.

"No." Aim's voice wavers slightly.

Raising my hands, I begin to form a shield around us. Aim follows suit. Used to working together, our magic melds seamlessly, creating an invisible bubble around us. A blue shimmer sparks in the light before it goes translucent. Moving forward, we scan the rapidly darkening area. The temperature plummets, and a cloud forms in front of my mouth. My flesh pimples as a chill sets in. Fog rolls in, covering our feet and moving up to mid-calf. I began to feel disoriented. Aim grabs my hand.

"Stop. Something's wrong."

Inhaling, I breathe out slowly, grounding myself. "Something is trying to throw us off."

"It's powerful to manipulate the environment like this," Aim whispers.

The wind picks up, rustling the leaves overhead and sending in more fog. "Strengthen the shield." Tightening the leash on our magic, we push the otherworldly fog out. The ground trembles beneath our feet, and the air becomes a hazy blur as a misty rain begins to fall. We move to stand back to back. A streak of lightning illuminates the sky above us. A loud boom of thunder erupts above our heads, and I nearly jump out of my skin as the ozone raises, standing the hairs on my arms and the back of my neck on end.

Untapped power swells around us. Wind whistles through the trees, drawing my gaze up. My jaw drops as bodies bundled in a filmy white gauze tumble through the air to dangle from the branches of the trees just above us.

Pale faces with blue lips and shrunken cheekbones peer out from under their encasement.

"What are they wrapped in?" I whisper quietly.

Click, clack. Click, clack. Spindly legs appear from the haze, followed by a massive black thorax and abdomen. A pale, angular face with large, pupil-less beady eyes tops the strange entity.

"Jorogumo," I whisper.

"Translation, please." Aim's voice wavers.

"Spiderwoman. What the hell would she be doing here?"

"About to have a snack," Aim hisses.

The spiderwoman smacks her lips. Drool pours from the side of her mouth.

"She can't be real."

She bares her fangs in response. Strands of salvia stretch to fill her gaping mouth.

"She looks pretty damn real to me."

Throwing her arms back, the spiderwoman shoots a deluge of white webbing. The strands slap against our shield. Off-kilter, we stagger back as our bubble is rocked. The white strands tighten around us. My knees weaken and my eyes grow heavy.

"She's draining our energy," Aim cries. Suddenly, the attacks make sense. She's gathering the life force of others. *That's not what Jorogumo do. They live to eat the flesh, particularly of men. I saw the faces of women in the webs.* The pieces don't fit together. Picturing a razor-sharp knife, I send out a blast of fuchsia energy to slice through the web. They glowed with dark energy as the spiderwoman cackled and absorbed it like a parched person in the rain.

Aim follows me with a blue spray of magic, that resembles bullets. The spiderwoman stumbles back. We tense, ready to follow up the assault when her body shimmers, and she grows larger.

"What the hell?" Aim screams.

"Japanese monsters require Japanese banishing," I murmur. Digging into my satchel, I pull out a strip of hemp cloth with kanji blessed by a shrine and wrapped in a decorative bag to be portable I send out a prayer to whoever might be listening. Removing the paper from the bag, I take a deep breath.

"Cover me and close the barrier behind me."

"No. You can't go out there."

Slipping through the sliver I've opened in our shield, I hold up the ofuda dedicated to the Sun Goddess, Amaterasu.

Legs stab downward toward the earth. I jump back, narrowly missing the spray of webbing that lands millimeters from me, coating the spot I once stood. The spiderwoman charges forward, and I stand my ground.

"Dispel this darkness," I bark the command, feeling the ofuda charge. Tossing it with my hand, I channel my best gambit and direct the glowing strip with my powers onto the center of the spiderwoman's forehead. An explosion lifts me off my feet. My ears ring, as my mind goes blank. An impact jolts me awake. I force my heavy lids up and find myself staring down at grass-covered earth. Moving my shaky arms beneath me, I force myself up and spit out dirt and moss.

"Ez." Aim kneels beside me. "Are you okay?"

"I think so." I scrub my mouth to get rid of the speckles of earth. "What happened?"

"She turned into an arts and crafts project."

I close my eyes. "She was a messenger. The main boss has yet to be revealed. A shikigami is a minion, bound to its master, and they do their bidding. Formed from magic and paper, they can only be created by a powerful sorcerer adapt in the ancient art of Onmyodo."

"For what end?" She shakes her head.

"To gather power."

Thump, thump. The bodies hit the ground. I flinch. Sitting up, I catch my breath as Aim scans the limp bodies sprawled out on the ground. "They're in various stages of death."

A curved ear catches my attention. Forcing myself onto my feet, I walk over to the alabaster skinned being who radiates a strange type of magic. As his glamour melts away, two antlers protrude from his head. A golden crown of mulberry leaves stands out against his light blond hair.

"He's a royal."

Aim whistles. "We're duty-bound to help by the treaty. He's looking bad."

His chest rises and falls slightly. "He must've been a prize. The energy of a fae is incomparable to just about anything else." I hold my hand over his body and close my eyes, tracking his life force. "He's in the in-between. I can reach him and bring him back *if* he corporates."

"You work on him, and I'll deal with the others."

I can feel the time slipping away for them. They've been drained for an indeterminable amount of time, and they're exhausted. With every second, they move closer to the great beyond. Blocking out the souls crying out to be saved, I focus on the one closest to me. Locking onto his signature, I dive through the layers of consciousness and dimensions, following his faintly glowing life force. Everyone's death experience is different depending on their belief system. There is no one blanket system.

I find myself entering a lush, green forest. Bright flora and fauna line the golden path that winds through the trees. Continuing to follow his signature, I find myself in front of a large tree of life. The trunk is massive, and the branches reach farther than my eyes can track.

"You're the first person I've seen since I arrived. I catch glimpses of people in the distance, but when I go to find them, they aren't there."

I turn and find the boy restored to his usual splendor. Porcelain skin shimmers as if lit from within. His silver eyes are mercurial and bright beneath his thick, pale blond brows. His face is perfectly symmetrical, and his lips form a cupid bow. The flawless features do nothing to hide the cruel set of his mouth or the murder in his eyes. This was a dangerous being.

"Because you're not dead yet. You have one foot in the land of the living and a toe in the land of the dead."

"And you're what? The grim reaper?" He eyes me disdainfully. "I hate to say it, but I expected something more regal." His lip curls up, in direct contrast with the ethereal sound of a voice. He's an angel that would lead you straight into the darkness.

I laugh. "I'm the necromancer who freed you from the spiderwoman's web."

"She's dead?" He blinks, clearly stunned. Inclining his head, he acknowledges the accomplishment.

"She is. She was a spirit set to do the bidding of her master. I'm curious." I consider my words carefully. If he finds me to be offensive it could lead to us both being hurt. The Fae aren't known for their compassion. "How did she lure you in?"

"Her song. She had the most beautiful voice I'd ever heard. I wanted to take her home to my court. But when I got close enough to see the beautiful woman in a white dress, she spun her web around me. The harder I fought, the more powerful she became. The fight was over before it truly began, and I lost consciousness."

"Do you know how long ago that was?"

He arches a delicate brow. "What is time to a being like me?"

"Right. So we have no clue how long you've been MIA. A lot's probably happened since you've been away. We're approaching a Night Hunt."

His silver eyes narrow. "Do tell."

"The rules have changed. The boundaries that separated our worlds are thinning, and predators are slipping through. The ghostly spectrals are upsetting the natural order, During the chaos, everyone's making a play for power and control. I'm not convinced the spiderwoman isn't linked to that."

His lips form a flat line. "I see. Someone's gotten greedy. I need to check on my court."

"If you put your trust in me, I can guide you back, but it'll be painful."

He laughs. "What's a bit of pain for a favorable outcome? Do what you need to, necromancer."

I place my palms together, gathering my energy, and grip his wrist. Energy crackles around us. "Hold on."

His screams follow me into the abyss as I navigate my way through the in-between to the present realm.

His silver eyes open, and I lean back, breathing heavily as weariness floods through my body.

"I find myself in your debt, necromancer."

"Ezra."

He smirks. "Ezra then. You may call me Prince Bayard of the Winter Court. Now at your service, I suppose." Peering around, Bayard frowns. "I've had my fill of this place. Let us take our leave."

Looking over at Aim, who looks dazzled, I feel my gut clench. Humans mixing with the fae never ends well.

"You weren't the only one in need of rescuing … Your Highness," Aim says with a curtsey.

"Marvelous! Manners." Bayard claps his hands. "I believe I can help with this. Where would you like them?"

"We hadn't gotten that far yet," I admit.

"To the basement of the Parlor. We'll let Lazarus contact the right people."

"Done." Prince Bayard snaps his fingers, and suddenly we appear in the middle of the bustling restaurant.

Silence fell as heads turn, and a low whisper begins.

"You sure know how to make an entrance," Frida says sarcastically.

"We found a few things in the forest."

"I noticed." Frida turns to the other witches flanking her. "Let's get them in the back and start untangling this mess."

CHAPTER NINE

Shouldn't we stay and help them?" Waylon gestures toward the group of people all speaking at once.

"Nope. I'm leaving the politics to them. Right now, my job is finding out who put all these people in this position and how to get the upper hand on the huntsmen."

"I—" She glanced back at the group, and I took a moment to start weaving my way through the crowd. Unlike her, my loyalties aren't split. The Coalition called for all hands on deck to return the injured parties to their rightful places. With the remnants of the shikigami in my pocket, I was headed to the one person who could shine a light on the ancient magic used to animate it. Aunt Hisa's best friend and shop owner, Mrs. Tanaka.

The old widow sold powders, potions, and charms out the back of her shop while supplying the rest of the town with herbs and other Asian specific goods. The nice sized Asian population kept her shop alive and well. I stepped on the stairs to head out the back, and a hand wrapped around my arm.

"We're supposed to be doing this together," Waylon states.

"If you feel you should be here, I'd understand. I mean, all your people are here trying to get this situation sorted out."

"Don't pretend to care about me. You're not getting rid of me that easily." She glares.

I shrug. "Suit yourself. Just keep up and do what I tell you."

"Yeah, that's not going to happen."

"This isn't your world, Waylon. Where we're going, there are traditions to be observed, and respect that needs to be given."

"I can follow your lead without being a mute."

"We get one shot at this. It's bad enough that I'm bringing in an outsider." The words may seem harsh, but it doesn't make them any less true. Mrs. Tanaka is old school, like her practices. Which is good for gathering information. Not so much for making new friends.

"My job is to help you. Frida saw it. You're going to need me."

The words make me flinch. "I'll never need you, Waylon."

"The seer says otherwise."

Grinding my teeth, I choke back the responses dying to fly free. My jaw ticks and my grip tightens on the banister. "Be careful with that train of thought. Prophecies don't always unfold the way you expect."

She steps onto the stair beside me, refusing to back down. "And yet, they *do* come to pass."

Our gazes clash. Her breath caresses my face. The floral scent that's always clung to her teases my nostrils. Practically vibrating with rage, she's every bit as beautiful as she was when I first met her, and I hate it. My pride won't let me walk away. That would mean backing down. I can't afford to give even a millimeter where she's concerned.

"Is this how humans communicate nowadays?"

The haughty tone breaks the stalemate. We turn and find Bayard standing behind us.

"Prince Bayard, I was just heading out."

"*We* were," Waylon adds.

"I find myself bored by the melee happening below. You two seem to be on a mission. I shall accompany you."

How do you say no to royalty? "I don't think that's such a good idea."

He blinks as if he'd never heard the words spoken to him before. "I'm sorry, did you say no?"

"You don't exactly blend in, Prince Bayard, and we're going somewhere where making waves is frowned upon."

Sighing, he runs his fingers through his locks. "Yes, I am quite the distraction. Fear not, necromancer, I'm not without my tricks." White-blond hair turns to a dull dishwater blond, and silver eyes turn a dim blue-gray. His face morphs to be less perfect—a crooked smile, larger eyes, and thin lips. "I shall remain here until I've gathered enough information to return home. Even now, my spies are at work."

"Didn't take you long."

"That's why I've remained on top for so long. We don't pretend to be ruthless the way you are here, so there's never a need to be surprised when you're stepped on by the next person trying to make it to the top of the ladder." He claps his hand. "Now. We should be off. I'm in need of entertainment, and you were doing … well, what were you doing?" The corners of his mouth turn down.

"Investigating the spiderwoman."

His eyes flash silver. The fury visible dries my throat out. "Oh, then I am most definitely accompanying you."

I open my mouth and close it, shaking my head. I don't have time to fight a battle I know I'm going to lose. It's not wise to anger a fae, and this one is royalty. No isn't a word he'll understand.

"Night's wasting, and the shop won't be open much

longer." Giving them my back, I plod up the stairs wondering how the hell I ended up here and where my aunt disappeared to. It wasn't like her not to see things through. Maybe she doesn't have a choice where she is. Apprehension settles in my chest like water seeping up to clog my breathing. Things are amiss and I need to figure out why.

A fairy, a vampire, and a necromancer climb into a car. It sounds like the punch line to a joke, but somehow, it's my life. The air inside of the car is heavy as the unresolved argument lingers. Turning on the radio to discourage any attempt at conversation, I crank the volume and flirt with the speed limit. I don't want to be sandwiched between the two problems any longer than I have to be.

"Dull. Tell me your story." The words are more command than request.

"Not much to tell. I speak with the dead for a fee."

"Oh, no, you're no simple death magic wielder. I can see the magic coming off you in waves." Bayard sniffs. "I can smell it."

"Human 101, Prince, it's rude to mention how people smell," Waylon says.

"Why? It was a compliment. He's no one to be trifled with. Though I'm not sure he's realized it yet." He sniffs again. "You are a different store. There's a darkness hidden behind that unassuming appearance."

"You don't know what you're talking about."

His brittle laughter sets me on edge. "Girl, I *am* the darkness." The sky darkens, and thunder booms directly over the car. "Winter Court is Unseelie. Like knows like." His words and casual use of power draw my attention.

"Now this is entertaining, Prince Baylard. Please continue."

"You know nothing," Waylon says darkly.

"Oh, I know plenty, Lovecraft."

"That is not who I am anymore."

"Isn't it? Do you think you can block out all the things you've done with a change of surname?"

Waylon turns away, refusing to comment.

What did she do?

"Everyone's secrets have a price, necromancer. Be sure you're ready to pay before you ask." The prince leans forward. "Unless you want to cash in your favor now."

"I'll hold on to it."

"Hmmm." Baylard flounces into the back seat, draping over the bench like it's a settee from the Victorian Era.

"The veil is thin here. I can feel the otherworld just on the other side." Baylard taps the window and moves his face closer to the window. The tapping echoes through the car, growing louder. Tap. Tap. Tap. "I can almost feel the vibrations running through my body." Tap. A final tap shifts the energy around us. The atmosphere warps, and the landscape changes. Large, dark trees blot out a gray sky. The tires roll over a wooden bridge.

"What happened?"

"We're in my realm," Baylard says, immediately alert. Sitting up straight up, he rolls down the window.

"Why?" Waylon asks.

"When I figure that out, I'll tell you," Baylard relies.

Back on land, I marvel at the impossible twisted trees and jagged rock structures that seem to spring up haphazardly. In the distance, a horn blows.

"I see. It's not me they're after."

"The huntsmen," I whisper.

"If you can make this metal bucket go faster, I suggest you do it. I'll work on getting us back."

Dust rises from the road as the thunder of hooves grows louder. The ground trembles. Sweat beads on my brow and upper lip. My hands clutch the steering wheel while I press the gas pedal down. The speed presses me back into my seat. I watch the bar on the speedometer fly to the right. We fly past one hundred, and the unseen enemy continues to gain on us. My chest aches as the intense sensation of evil, oily and sticky, encompasses me. This is more than death, it is corruption, rage, and hate that burns hotter than lava. Glowing red eyes appear from the dirt cloud as the figures began to take shape.

A large frame with shoulders that would put the best

linebacker to shame emerges darker than the night that had fallen. Moonlight reveals large arms encased in dark armor, covered in black vines and a rusted helmet, open to show the searing gaze fixed on us. Spikes sprout out from the shoulders and wrists, promising to dole out pain. Their black steeds are foaming at the mouth and have the same unholy red embers for eyes. Their nostrils breathe smoke, and their coats seem to glisten in the moonbeams. One draws a bow. The arrow flies through the air, whistling before it hits the back window and shatters the glass. Stray pieces nick the side of my face and my neck. Swerving to the right, I try to make us a harder target.

Two more arrows came through the back window. Waylon screams as smoke pours from her wound.

"Holy water!" She yanks the arrow free.

"Baylard."

"It seems someone has been helping themselves to my power back home. They knew I was trapped. I'll have to rectify that." Waving his hand, he replaces the glass. The arrows bounce off his newly reinforced barrier. "This will hold for now." He places his hands together, and a crack forms in the darkness up ahead. "I'll make sure they do not follow. You get us through the opening."

The car lifts from the ground as hooves come down on the trunk.

"Not today." Baylard flicks his wrist, sending the huntsman crashing into its kin.

Willing the car to go faster, I press the toe of my boot into the floorboard, boosting the car with my powers. The car jerks to the right as the driver's window explodes. Screaming at the white-hot pain that explodes in my shoulder, I refuse to be deterred. I cast the assailant aside with my mind, grit my teeth, and focus on the light up ahead amidst the darkness. Drifting into the white light as my vision blurs, I feel my body jerk while we pass through the veil and land on the other side.

When the car slams down onto the ground, I lose control. Veering into the ditch, I curse, my shoulder throbbing.

"Ezra." The worry in Waylon's voice is frightening. I don't want her to care about me.

"It's just a flesh wound." I glance down at the lance embedded in my flesh and try not to pass out when I see how much blood has soaked through my shirt. My body temperature has dropped, and I shiver as a chill sets in.

"That needs to come out," Waylon says.

"You think?"

"Are you really going to argue with me?" Waylon barks.

"Why change things up now?" I scoff.

"Because you're bleeding out."

"I'd wager it won't be long before someone comes along on this road and wonders why you're in this situation," Baylard says. When a fae is the voice of reason, things have gone wrong.

"Hold still." Waylon grasps the lance and tugs.

I scream as my muscles tense and the wood gives. I bring my hand up to press against my wound.

"I can heal this," Waylon says.

"No." I shove her hand away. "I need my satchel." Digging inside of the worn leather, I find the fire agate. Wrapping my blood-slicked hand around the smoky orange and white stone, I press it into my wound and connect to the fire inside. I jerk against the blinding agony that forces my eyes shut. My body jerks as the skin is cauterized.

Gasping for air, I come down from my haze. My hand trembles as I wave it over myself, cleaning the shirt. Winded, I rest my head against the steering wheel.

"Stubborn fool," Waylon spits.

"Impressive," Baylard whispers.

Ignoring the exhaustion that makes me want to go home and crawl into bed, I hand the lance to Baylard. "Tell me what you can about this." Inhaling deeply, I release the breath and pull the idling car back onto the road.

"You are not okay," Waylon chides.

"Is anyone?" I ask.

The small shop looks just as I remember it from the outside. Sandwiched between two bigger buildings, the glass window with Kanji writing in gold and the words 'Spice Shop' is easy to miss if you're not looking for it. Opening the door, I step inside as the bells jingle overhead. Spices and incense blend to create a unique scent that takes me back to my youth.

The petite woman with graying-black hair cut in a bob that frames her round face smiles. "Ezra."

"Mrs. Tanaka." I bow and walk toward her.

"It's good to see you." The smile drops from her face. "Come with me." Her steps are sure and still quick for a woman pushing mid-seventies.

Following behind her without question, I wave the others to follow me. We move through the beaded curtain to the back of the shop.

"Sit." She gestures toward a stool, and I do her bidding.

"What's happening?" Waylon asks.

Mrs. Tanaka turns her dark gaze to Waylon and wags her finger. "You still haven't learned your lesson?"

"We're actually here on business."

"Hmmm. So you say." Grabbing a large, gray mortar and pestle, she begins to gather odds and ends from the shelves. "You've seen them, the riders in black. They're returning to destroy and kill."

143

"Yes. That's why we've come here. Today we battled a shikigami that posed as a spiderwoman."

Pausing in mid-pour, Mrs. Tanaka sucks her teeth. "That's not good. It takes a powerful person to create a shikigami, but to create such an elaborate one …" She shakes her head.

"Do you have any clue who might be practicing the old ways?" I shift in my seat. Heat radiates from inside of me, and I notice the line of sweat on my brow and upper lip. I push myself past the weariness threatening to overcome me.

She looks thoughtful. "I can ask around and see what I pick up. These matters are usually kept secret."

"But you know likely candidates."

She hums. "Maybe."

"What exactly are you doing?" Baylard asks.

"Saving his life," she replies nonchalantly.

"What?" I croak.

"You've come into contact with something toxic. Even now, it's flowing through your veins."

My vision blurs, and I blink to clear it. "Are you sure?"

"It's dark, like a nasty black sludge covering your natural aura." Mrs. Tanaka shudders. "Everything else will have to wait." Done mixing the concoction together, she hands me the bowl. "Drink."

Swallowing it down, I ignore the bitter taste.

She rushes away, and returns with water and a dipper. "Hold out your hands." She washes the left and then the right, before pouring more for me to drink. I recognize the cleansing ritual as I sway slightly. Lighting incense, she grabs a hairaigushi. The white paper strip covered stick is a purification wand. Waving it over me, she chants as the world blurs.

Gripping the edge of the table to keep from toppling forward and smashing my face, I close my eyes to try to keep my balance. There's a war going on inside of me as fire and ice clash. Shivering and sweating, I let my head drop to my chest.

I slip into an odd state of consciousness that feels like being underwater. I have one foot in the real world and another somewhere else. I can hear Mrs. Tanaka in the distance, but all I see is blackness.

"Ezra." I spin around, searching for the source of the sound. My name is distorted, like it's being filtered through a voice distortion box.

"Ezra." The voice comes from my left now.

Spinning, I turn toward it. A light flickers. I lift my hand to shield my sensitive retinas. A moment later, the brightness dims, and I make out Aunt Hisa.

"Where have you been?"

"You have to be careful, Ezra. She—"

She flickers out, and I'm left in darkness once more.

"Hisa." Spinning around, I panic. *Who is she?*

My stomach drops. *Run.*

Following my instinct, I take off into the darkness, feeling like the hounds of hell are nipping at my ankles, and breathing down my neck. Pumping my arms, I pick up the pace. Lungs burning, my heart threatens to leap from my chest. *Don't stop. Don't slow down.* I stumble, tripping and falling. I sink through the abyss, passing through layers of darkness that grow thicker and thicker, wrapping around me and squeezing like a boa constrictor. Gasping for breath, I struggle against the unseen force. Woozy, I feel my head nod.

Out of time, I let the dark take me.

CHAPTER TEN

Coolness drapes over my forehead, easing the heat. Sighing, I slowly open my heavy lids. Waylon's bright brown eyes earn a slow smile.

"You're awake," she whispers.

"Yes." Suddenly, the present catches up with me, and I press my lips into a flat line.

"Where's Mrs. Tanaka?"

"She went to see the Itako."

I sit up straight. "Are you sure you heard her correctly?"

"Yes?"

I glance down at the small cot. "Where's the prince?"

"He took her. She said it was far away."

"That's an understatement. Itako are blind women

trained to be mediums in a small area of Japan. Nearly extinct, they can only be found in the mountains of Aomori."

"Oh."

"How long was I out?"

"About six hours. You should lay back down." She pushes at my chest.

"There's no time for that."

"Well, regardless, we're stuck here for now. The sun's up."

"No, you're stuck here." I pull away from her.

"Ezra, you can't leave me here by myself. I don't know her or this area."

"We're wasting valuable time."

"What else is there to do now, but wait for them to get back?"

Sighing, I run my fingers through my hair. It's my worst nightmare being trapped in a small space with her. "Working on leads."

"Okay, so let's do that." She places the cold compress on the nightstand beside me.

"I saw my aunt while I was unconscious."

"Hisa?"

I give a quick nod. "She tried to warn me about her."

"Who?"

I huff. "I don't know. That's all she got out before something blocked her."

"In your dreams?"

"I think so. It takes a powerful person to manipulate spirits like that. Especially someone as strong as my aunt. I think there are multiple things happening here. I'm just not sure if they're related."

"It's suspicious timing if they aren't."

"Yeah." I lean my head back against the wall and close my eyes. It's a puzzle, and I don't have all the pieces. "What happened while I was out?"

"She prayed over you, burned incense, and told me to keep your temperature down, so I've been using cold compresses. You tossed, and turned, and mumbled." She looks at the wall behind me. A haunted expression settles over her face. "I preferred that to the stretches of silent stillness."

Her obvious emotions are unsettling. "Well, I'm better now, and we've got work to do." I ignore the desperate longing for a shower, and force my brain to do a quick reboot. "Did you check in with Lazarus?"

She nods. "Yeah, he told me to keep him posted. I'll let him know you're up and functioning."

"What happened last night with the returns?"

"Seems your rescue fostered the beginning of peace talks."

"That's good." At least something came out of the ass-kicking I'd been treated to. "We're going to need all the friends we can get."

"They're coming together later tonight to discuss the Wild Hunt's return. There have been more incidents." She stumbled over the words.

"Incidents?"

"The dogs have been seen again, and some swear they heard the sound of the horn in the distance." She twists her lips together. "Do you think they heard it while we were there? That the break occurred in other places?"

"I think it might've spilled over," I admit.

"Things are unraveling fast."

"They always do."

"I had a lot of time to think over the past few hours, and I can't pass up my second chance to set things straight."

"I've already heard your reasons, Waylon. We don't have to rehash them."

"No." She places a hand on my chest, and my heart kicks up a notch. "I have more to say, and right now, you have to listen to me because there's nowhere to run."

"I'm not running."

"Yes, you are, and I let you. No more. We could've died earlier, and I would've taken this to my grave. I never stopped loving you."

The words are a knife to the gut. "N—"

She covers my mouth with her hands. "Regardless of what you may think, I've never fallen out of love with you. There hasn't been anyone else. There never could be when you have my heart. I made the only choice I felt I could at the time. In hindsight, I wish I had handled things differently."

Grabbing her wrists, I force her hands away. "You denied our entire relationship in front of everyone, Waylon. After I'd given up my family and my home to be with you. You can't fix that."

"I know. But it doesn't mean we can't start over."

"Waylon," I snap.

"Tell me there are no more feelings between us, and I'll let this drop."

"There are plenty of feelings—"

Her lips pressing against mine make my mind go blank. Tilting her head, she snakes her tongue out to tease my lips apart and slips inside. Reacting on instinct, I open up and join the duel. We thrust and parry, fighting like fencers. My hand creeps up to bury in her curls, and for a second, we're just Waylon and Ezra again. The two peas in a pod who liked the same geeky things, only had eyes for each other, and fit together seamlessly. My lids lower and fire spreads through my veins. Unable to stop the passion that's been uncorked, I deepen the kiss, gripping her hip I pull her closer. Her flowery scent intoxicates me, slowing my response time and drugging my senses.

Her fingertips tickle the nape of my neck, and I shiver. Parting for air, we stare at each other, dumbfounded.

"You still taste the same." She runs her fingertips over her lips, reverently.

"You shouldn't have done that."

"I never heard you say you felt nothing."

"Because I'm not a liar. I might not be able to control the way I feel, but I can control my actions. I'm not going there again with you, Waylon."

She drops her head. "Never say never. It's a strange world out there."

"This isn't helping anyone."

"It helped me." Her voice is almost too low to hear.

Must be nice, because now I'm confused as hell.

"We have a job to do, Waylon. Once it's completed, I'm gone."

"I know."

Do you?

"Let's go back to the case. I need to look at the book to try to bring back the night warriors. I know little more than whispers at this point."

She gestures to the books behind her. "There are plenty of books here."

"It's a starting point at least."

"Yes, but I don't read Japanese."

"Then I guess you'll have to stick to the ones in

English." The separation between us pleases me. I need to get my bearings and rebuild my resolve.

Pushing up from the cot, I lock my knees to keep from falling back. I bend over, and hear my spine pop as I reach down and touch my toes. Loosening stiff muscles, I walk over to the shelf and skim the spines. Welcoming the silence, I pick a few older volumes and sit back on the cot to comb through it. Volume after volume, I search for any mention of the aloof beings who stood firm against the Night Huntsmen. A counterpart, the Night Warriors, were made to even the playing field, though I wasn't sure how they were created. I have my suspicions. Dark magic, or the fae. They love a good contest, and a counterbalance to the Night Huntsmen would make their length of service last longer and adds unpredictability to the situation.

"I think I found something," Waylon says. "Born from desperation, these warriors are the final line of defense against the hunters who stalk in the night, killing magical beings without discrimination because they hate all who are other than them."

"Let me see that." Setting aside my book, I walk over and take the leather-bound book from her hands. A triangle with a line through and across it connected by a circle that looks like a joint is printed below. The sigil is the key to summoning them forth once more.

"Jackpot."

"You got it?"

"I think so." My mind begins to spin as I try to implement a plan. "This is going to take a lot of juice to pull off. If I can ever figure out where to summon them."

"Didn't you say the book acted like a GPS for the dead?" Waylon questions.

"I did." *I wonder what else the good book has to say about Night Warriors.* Picturing my aunt's library, I know home is where I need to be. I glance at Waylon.

She points her finger at me. "Don't even think about it."

"What?" I ask, baffled.

"Leaving me."

I hold up my hands. "I didn't say a word."

"You didn't have to."

"We've done everything we can here."

"Not yet." She slams a book called *The Diary of a Founder of Snoqualmie* into my chest. "Keep reading. The more we know about our enemy the better prepared we can be. I get the feeling this isn't your average historical account."

Taking the thick tome from her, I flip it up, stunned by the almost journal-style listing of events and creatures. "You're two for two, Waylon. "

"Maybe I'm not so bad to have around, huh?"

I grunt noncommittally and continue to flip through the pages that chronicle major events that have happened.

"Listen to this. They all gathered. Night dwellers, magic casters, and moonwalkers alike to face off against the ravenous riders, who'd see them all dead." I tap the shadowy drawing sketched on the next page. "They're talking about the Night Huntsmen."

"What else does it say?" Moving in, she leans closer to read along with me. "They gathered in the place where the veil was worn thin and pledge their life's essence."

"A blood pact, maybe?" I mutter.

"Doing the deal with the trickster, they were born of earth, magic, and blood. Rising from the dirt, magnificent and strong. The fiery ones were a light to combat the darkness. A hope for stopping the mindless slaughter that plagued us for centuries."

"This is what we know. Our ancestors grew fed up with the loses, and utter ruin the huntsmen caused. It forced them to come together to create the Night Warriors. I don't understand why they wouldn't rise with the Huntsmen, as they have before," Waylon says softly.

"Because the huntsmen are playing under new rules, and magic can weaken over time. Given the divide, I think the friction between us all rendered the spell null and void. The trust entered into in order to make them is all but gone."

"So, what do we do?" she asks.

"I'm still working on an answer to that," I admit honestly.

The beads of the curtain clack together as Mrs. Tanaka and Prince Baylard enter. "The blood of those who called forth the warriors must be spilled before they can return," Mrs. Tanaka states. "We cannot prevent the hunt. This is meant to happen. It's rebirth. If we stick together, we can overpower the huntsmen and banish them to the depths of the earth where they belong."

My shoulders slump. "We're going to war then?"

"Yes. And we must be prepared. Rally the troops, raise the cry, and unite the old families because the time is near. When the full moon rises, the veil will fall and the game will be afoot once more."

The more I hear about this, the less I want to be involved.

"I've done some recon, and it appears my dear brother, Durin, has been a busy worker bee and ascended the throne that should've been mine. We all knew Father was grooming me to take his place. Durin never had the spine to do what needed to be done."

Apparently, he found it.

"I underestimated him. It was a nearly fatal mistake. The lands are under his control for now."

"Wouldn't they know you weren't dead?" Waylon asks.

"Not if magic is involved." Prince Baylard frowns. "It seems the spiderwoman was a cleverly laid trap. I've got a score to settle with my brother. I will pay him back in kind." He balls his hand into a fist. "When the time is right. For now, I will help you here as I gather new allies. Ones whose loyalty is not in question."

"You think others knew?"

"Promises of riches, renown, and power could tempt saints, and we both know my people are anything but holy." He chuckles. "I'm impressed. Who knew he had it in him?"

"You look proud."

"Oh, I am. I can appreciate a well-executed plan. He did well. I'll do better." The determined glint in his eyes chills the blood in my veins. "For now, we have a message to deliver, and since you have me, we'll be heard and re-vered." He waves his hand with flourish.

"You don't know the state of relationships between the vampires, witches, and werewolves if you believe that," Waylon remarks.

"None of that matters when we're talking about sur-vival. You'd do well to remember that." He sniffs. "First things first. We need to make you look presentable."

Glancing down, I'm acutely aware of how badly I need to shower.

"Mrs. Tanaka, thank you for everything you've done." I bow respectfully.

"You were my best friend's heartbeat. Whatever I am

able to do to assist you, I will. This is bigger than us, however. I fear for our community if we continue along the path we've created." She shakes her head. "The contempt, hate, bickering, and segregation will be our final downfall. People have forgotten they're stronger together. You must remind them of that."

"Me?" Placing a hand on my chest, I shake my head back and forth. "No. This isn't a role I'm meant to play."

"We don't get to pick and choose our destiny. I know you young people believe fate is yours to determine, but some things once set in motion can't be undone, or de-railed."

Her words burn like a branding iron, permanently tying me into the situation.

"Your family's legacy lives on in you." She presses a hand over my heart. "You are more than your mother's child. You belong to your father, your aunt, and your ancestors. Do you understand?"

Energy surrounds me, re-energizing, and reassuring me. For a moment, I smell my father's familiar cologne. My family is rallying around me.

"I do," I whisper. To deny my lot in life because of my mother is to also reject them. I'm an elder.

"It is time you become the man your aunt and I always knew you could be."

"I'll do my best, Auntie," I say, using the term of endearment and respect for elders.

The building rocks and a loud bang sounds. Thrown off-balance, I stumble. Waylon's hand shoots out and rights me.

"What's happening?"

"We're under attack," Mrs. Tanaka relies. "This place is magically protected. I don't think they were counting on that."

The ground vibrates. Reaching out, I grab Mrs. Tanaka to keep her steady.

"Who would do this?" Waylon inquires.

"I'm checking the wards now."

"Shikigami," Mrs. Tanaka whispers.

"Shit." Images of the spiderwoman and her sisters haunt my mind.

"She won't try to do the same thing twice." Mrs. Tanaka clucks her tongue. Rushing to the window, we peer outside and find two large, red-skinned ogres with two horns protruding from their bulbous foreheads. Fiery red eyes gaze from large eyes that rest over thin-lipped mouths. Peeled back, they reveal sharp teeth and two prominent fangs.

"Oni!'

"What?" Waylon asks.

"Japanese ogres," Prince Baylard says.

Lifting their large, black clubs, they bring the items back down on the shop. Sparks fly as magic meets magic.

"It'll only hold so long."

"How did they know we were here?" I ask.

"When you answer that question, we'll have our sorceress," Mrs. Tanaka states.

"How do we get rid of it?" Waylon asks.

"We send it back to where it came from." Mrs. Tanaka walks over to her shelf, pulls out a wooden box with gold Kaji, and sets it on the counter in front of her. Opening the lid, she reaches inside and removes a straw doll, crudely bound to resemble the human form. The wara ningyo makes my mouth dry. The cursed doll is dark magic, used to kill or destroy the receiver on the wrong end of the hex. She glances up and smiles. "This is not what you think. It's a doll of my own creation, made with protection amulets inside. It changes the intent of the Ushi no Taki Mairi ritual, and turns it into a powerful curse reversal."

"Does that work?" I ask skeptically.

"I haven't had cause to use it until today, so I suppose we'll find out together."

"I don't like the sound of this," Waylon deadpans.

"Let the woman work her magic," Prince Baylard says, clearly amused.

"Not all of us can pop out of a situation if the trouble gets too bad," Waylon says.

"I'm pretty sure your speed will let you run fast enough, vampire."

Waylon hisses, baring her fangs.

"Are you challenging me, fledgling?" Prince Baylard raises an eyebrow.

"We don't have time for this." Mrs. Tanaka's voice is firm. "Ezra, come and help me, please." She reaches inside another wooden box and pulls out a dried-out piece of wood. "I need you to bring it back for me. It's a piece of a holy tree I brought from Japan."

Inanimate objects are different, harder. Even though the tree was once alive, it's not like a human spirit. It takes a lot more concentration and effort. Focusing on the wood grain and the shape and weight, I coax the dried piece in my hand back to life and make it grow from a sapling to a baby tree, with a wide enough trunk to fit the straw doll.

"I need three white candles," Mrs. Tanaka says to Waylon as she grabs five nails from the counter and a hammer.

"Your Highness, a smudging if you will."

"How ancient magic of you." Snapping his fingers, he produces a bundle of burning sage. He did nothing without flourish. Waving his finger, he began to cleanse the area.

"I need all of you to imagine white light, encircling the building, strengthening the wards and forming a mirror for the oni to see their reflection in. Imagine their attack rebounding off that smooth, clear surface."

"Hold the doll still, Ezra." Lifting the first nail, she begins to speak in Japanese. "Return to your Maker, and leave us in peace. The way is barred, your power shall cease. Say it with me." Our voices raise in unison as the building threatens to tumble down around us. Glass shatters when a window gives. I feel the wards waver. The loud roar makes the hair on my neck stand on end.

"Keep going," Mrs. Tanaka yells.

We continue to chant as she hammers another nail in. The rounded tip of a bat is shoved through the jagged fragments of the window. The hammer taps the head of the final nail and a wall slams into place. The Oni scream as they're blown one way and us the other. My head smacks against the wall. Blinking away the stars that appeared behind my eyes, I glance around the room. Waylon lays on her back, arm extended. Rushing to her side, I feel my stomach bottom out as I scan her. She's weak but alive ... or unalive.

"I think we have a problem." Prince Baylard looks unflappable as usual in his black pants, a long-sleeved black blouse with gold threading, and black lace cuffs. Leaning against the wall, he nods toward the table where Mrs. Tanaka once stood.

"No." Running around the table, I kneel beside her pale form. "She's alive. Her pulse is steady." I gently tap her cheeks. "Mrs. Tanaka, can you hear me?"

No response. A shimmery white aura surrounds her, indicating a vibrant lifeforce, but there's a gap. A disconnection around her head.

"Something's wrong. We need to get her to a hospital."

"The spell was a powerful one, and she channeled a vast quantity of power. That comes with a price."

"Do you know what's happening here?" I ask him.

"Overload. She's tough. It would've killed most women her age."

"Will she recover?" I ask, thinking of her two children.

"That depends on her."

Waylon moans. Her hand twitches and a rustle of movement later, she's back on her feet. "What happened?"

"I think she hit her head and overexerted herself," I say.

"What are we going to do?" Waylon sways slightly as she kneels on her opposite side.

"Call an ambulance.

"Do you think that's a good ideal?" Waylon asks.

"I think it's the best one. Whoever this sorceress is, she's kept a low profile, and she should be licking her wounds if the rebound hit her, too." I reach into the satchel at my side and pull out my cellphone. Swearing, I call nine-one-one and prepare for red tape, and angry family members.

Inside of his office in the Coalition compound, Lazarus paces back and forth as Frida shuffles tarot cards nervously.

"You're certain we can't prevent the huntsmen from coming?" Lazarus asks.

"I've read the cards multiple times, and the seer agrees. I can't change what the cards say. I can only read them."

"I know. The future is rarely set in stone, so I'd hoped …" Trailing off, Lazarus runs a hand through his dark hair. Leaning against the wall I study the others. Waylon mirrors my stance on the opposite side of the wall, and Aim perches on a chair. With her hands placed daintily in her lap, she seems unruffled. I see the strain around her mouth and eyes. Baylard stands beside her looking like a knight guarding his queen. The positioning disturbs me.

"Things may shift as new things happen, but certain events are fixed points that can't be moved." Frida shakes her head.

"Finding everyone in the forest really gave us all common footing to build from. We're being pushed together. Maybe it's time we listen and take a note from the past. We'll use those grateful vibes to get our foot in the door and meet them in their own environment. I want people to set up meetings with leaders in two people groups of mixed combinations. Let's show them what the Coalition is all about—unity and cooperation."

"I'll start making phone calls," Frida says.

"You two go and speak with the necromancers and some of the vampires without a clan."

"And you think they'll be receptive to us?" I ask.

"Make them be."

"We won't let you down," Waylon says.

"Speak for yourself, vampire. I don't make promises I can't keep." *Unlike you.*

Pursing her lips, Waylon glares at me.

"While the children fight it out, I'll make inquiries of my own," Baylard says coolly.

"I thought you were laying low," I say, surprised by his one-eighty.

"Given my lengthy slumber, I think it's time I changed that, don't you?" He's gone in the next moment.

"Fairies, always so damn flighty," Lazarus mutters.

"We're lucky he wants to help us. Especially after what happened with Mrs. Tanaka. I'm still trying to smooth things over with their family. We don't need to be at odds with them.

"You keep working on that angle. Waylon, I want you to go with Ezra. I need to know where your people stand Necromancer."

"I'm not one of your Coalition members, Lazarus."

He tenses. I straighten my back and stand firm. He could take my head off with one blow, but I know he needs me too much to do that.

"I never said you were." The words are clipped and laced with annoyance.

"You were doing a lot of ordering and very little asking. I *will* do what it takes to keep the town safe, as long as you remember I agree to do it for my own purposes. Not to ingratiate myself to you." I glance over at Waylon.

A growl rumbles in her chest, and she sneers.

"Is this going to be a problem?" Lazarus asks.

Her face blanks, and she shakes her head from side to side. "No, Lazarus."

Still following the orders of others, and not thinking for yourself. That's what tore us apart in the first place. Disgusted, I turn my head away. "I'll put the word out and get everyone together. We don't keep the same hours, and there's a lot of travel for work. I can send out an emergency signal, but it'll take a little time to rally. When I have more information, I'll contact Waylon and we can go visit them together."

Waylon steps in front of me. "And until then?"

"Is my business." I brush by her, ignoring the hole her heated gaze is burning into the back of my head.

Chapter Eleven

I shift my weight on the surprisingly comfortable rose-
pink couch with furry light pink pillows in the center
of the living room. We're in Aim's domain now and the
aesthetic is just as vibrant and feminine as her clothing.
A lace doily covers the round end table to the left of
me. Across from me in her hanging wicker chair with a
fuzzy white blanket over her lap she studied the slip of
parchment I handed her moments before.

  Her black booted foot, pushes off against the floor,
rocking her slowly back and forth. The white ruffled shirt
with a velvet bow around the neck and three black buttons almost blends in with the white design of the chair,
making the straps of her black jumper dress stand out.

"What am I looking at?" Aim lifts her gaze from the paper I've sketched the sigil on. Dark hair tumbles down around her shoulders, and the white bow bobs slightly as she leans forward.

"The Night Warrior's sigil."

Her jaw drops. "You found proof?"

I nod my head. "I did. The question is, what do I do with it?"

"You want to try to raise them?" she purses her lips and runs her fingers over the soft material of the blanket.

"I do. According to Mrs. Tanaka, it'll require the blood of the families that first made the blood pact." Her body tenses.

"Do you even know who that is?"

"I kind of got distracted in mid-research." I open the flap to my satchel. "Which is why I brought the book here."

"Where's your sidekick?" I try to read her evasive maneuver. Is she plucking me for information or stalling?

"I don't know." I shrug. "Trying to impress the Coalition probably."

"I'm shocked you got away from her." Her eyes narrow, and her attention centers directly on me.

"Are you trying to dig for info? Because I can reassure you, there's nothing there." I can't fault her for being concerned. I'd been a wreck for a long time after Waylon left.

"Then why are you blushing?" *My best friend the blood hound always sniffing out all the things I try to hide.*

"What?" My head shoots up. *Can she tell things have happened between Waylon and me?* Aim smirks. *Crap. I gave myself away.*

"Uh-huh. Spill it."

"She kissed me, and asked if we could start over." The words tumble out before I can stop them.

"Are you kidding me?" Aim screeches

"No." I exhale and hold up my hand. "I told her that was impossible after everything. That we were only associating now because it's literally a matter of life or death."

"Ez—" *Are her words tinged with disappointment?*

"Emotions can't be turned off and on like that," I snap. "If you want me to admit I still have feelings for her, of course I do. She was my first love. Hell, my only love, and things ended abruptly. So, no, I'm not over her. I might never be. I have to live with that. It doesn't mean I'm stupid enough to let her re-break my heart."

"Ezra," she whispers. The sadness in her tone leaves a sour taste in my mouth.

"No." I point at her. "Don't do that, Aim. Don't pity me."

She holds up her hands. "How can I not sympathize? You know I understand exactly how that feels. Ephraim disappeared, and I still think about him daily. The heart is a complex thing." Leaning over her end table, she grabs my hands. "It's okay to be human."

I swallow to moisten my dry mouth and push the lump in my throat down. "This is why I prefer the dead to the living."

"Ignore the fact that I want to kill her, and answer me honestly. Do you want to try again with her?"

"I can't even consider it. I've always been weak where she's concerned." My stomach knots as I remember the way I made a fool of myself that night.

Past

My chest tightens as I go over the speech I have prepared in my mind. I've been in love with Waylon nearly since the first moment I laid eyes on her. We cruised through our first year, persevered through the second year when my family tried to break us, and now that I've got my own place and independence, I'm ready to take the next step. I know we're young, but we both know what we want. Life's short, my father's death taught me that. So the last thing I want to do is wait. She's coming over tonight, and Aim is helping me get everything ready.

"You okay there, Ez?" Aim asks.

"Ask me after this is all over," I whisper.

She giggles. "Come on, you know she's going to say yes. Waylon's as crazy about you as you are her. You two are like a couple straight out of a manga." Sighing, she presses her hands together.

"Stop."

"What? You know I live vicariously through you."

"Like you and Ephraim aren't the same way?"

"No. we're just friends." She shakes her head.

"For now."

Her cheeks pinken, and I snicker. "Trust me. I know when a guy is into a girl. When you're not away at boarding school, he's constantly calling you, texting, or messaging."

"I don't know. He comes from a pretty strict family. They don't even like him attending the school from what he's said."

"That has nothing to do with his feelings for you."

"You think so?" She glances up at me, and I nod.

"I do. Any guy would be lucky to have you, Aim. Ephraim might just be worthy of the honor."

She grins. "Thanks, Ez." Straightening, her usual cheerful mood returns. She's like a birthday present in her bright purple jumper with layers of ruffles and white button-up with a Peter Pan collar. I know more than I ever wanted to about fashion. It's par for the course when your best friend in the world is a female this into Harajuku fashion. Her parents indulge her eccentrics, happy that her focus is on harmless things. I envy her close connection with them.

My mood darkens slightly. I haven't talked to my mother in six months since she told me to choose between her or Waylon. As if it was a contest. Once she booted me, I crashed with Aunt Hisa until I could find an apartment of my own a month later. I had the money I saved up from working at the shop, and it wasn't long before I was picking up small side gigs. Being a necromancer is a rare thing. It makes employment easy to obtain.

Aim carefully arranges the three white candles among the white and lavender Dahlias. The table is covered in white tealights, and more Dahlias that have been arranged around a wooden-letters—W and E. In the left-hand corner of the table is a birdcage with white pillar candles in the holders, and a black box. A large key rests on the end of the table.

"All right. You're all set up. I'm getting out of here before you lady love arrives."

"Thank you for this, Aim."

"Hey, when you're happy, I'm happy. You know that."

"Ditto." I squeeze her hand and walk her to the door. Shutting it behind her, I exhale.

Trying to keep busy, I straighten the house. Suddenly, a knock breaks the silence. *It's time.* Running to the door, I open it up.

"You're here." Taking her hand, I guide her inside.

"Ezra," her voice wavers, "what did you do?"

Kissing her hand, I bend down on one knee. "I know we're young—"

"Please don't do this," she whispers.

"What?" Her words are ice water dumped over my head. I lift my gaze and find her horrified expression. My stomach churns. "I don't understand."

"You can't. We can't." She stumbles over her words, trembling. "I came tonight to tell you we can't be together anymore. I'm sorry." Turning on her heels, she heads for the door. "Please don't follow me."

"Wait!" Springing up, I give chase as she speeds away using her vampiric powers. She's scared. After so long without anyone, I can understand that, but this isn't the answer.

Pounding down the steps, I find her halfway down the street with a group of vampires I've never seen before, all clad in black.

"Waylon." Panicked, I pick up the pace. They all pause, standing behind her, like silent watchers.

"Who are these people? Where are you going?"

She clenches her jaw and shakes her head, begging me for something I don't understand.

"We are her family," the tall man with pale skin and eerily light green eyes says.

"No. You're not. I've never even seen you before."

"Waylon, it's time we were going."

I reach out to grab her wrist, and find myself shoved back by the obvious leader. My chest screams, and I struggle to catch the breath he knocked out of me.

"Do you know this boy?" the man asks.

"No," she whispers.

The world around me stops. My ears fill with white noise, and I stare at the woman wearing my girlfriend's face and body. *No.*

Her eyes are devoid of emotion as she looks through me. "I've never seen him before in my life. He must be mistaken."

I stumble back as my world crashes down around me. My heart races, and I struggle to take in enough air as my vision begins to dim.

Present Day

"I gave up everything for her, gained my independence at seventeen, got a place, and just when I decided I wanted to spend the rest of my life with her, she left me without an explanation or a glance back. How can I ever reconcile that, no matter what her reasons are?"

"Only you can answer that question, Ez. All I want is to see you happy."

"I am."

"No, you're surviving not living, and I don't know how to change that." Her lower lip trembles.

"Aim?"

"I've been dreaming about Ephraim every night."

"Aww, Aim." I move over to sit beside her and pull her to my side. "I'm sorry. You deserved more."

"I don't think he left me of his own will. I can't help but think it was his family."

I want that to be the truth, but I'm too jaded. "You always said they were strange."

"I'm being stupid, aren't I?" She sniffs. "I should just move on and be done with it." Swiping away her tears, she tries to gather herself.

"Have you tried to search for him?" I trail my hand up and down her arm trying to warm a chill that has nothing to do with the temperature.

"No location spell ever took." Her voice wavers. "It's like he blinked out of existence."

"His family could be blocking you," I suggest gently. The alternative answer is too painful to consider. That Ephraim is dead.

"I know. How can I ever be okay when I can't get closure?"

"I don't know." I kiss her head, wishing I could take away the intense pain.

"Sorry for my meltdown." Clearing her throat, she pulls away and swipes at her eyes.

Ducking down, I force her to hold my gaze. "You never have to hide the way you feel from me."

"Thanks, E." She gives me a shaky smile. "Now, let's get us some Night Warriors."

"Yes, ma'am. You look over that book, and I'll look over this one." Removing the worn book I took from my home, I watch her eyes widen.

"The *Book of the Dead*," she says reverently.

Opening the tome, I begin to flip through the pages, unsure what I'm looking for. *If only this came with an instruction manual. Incantations. History. Summoning rituals.* Attention piqued, I carefully flip through the thin pages one by one, searching for any mention of the Night Warriors. The book vibrates, and the pages begin to give off a golden glow. Removing my hand, I watch in awe as the pages turn themselves before coming to a halt. Calling forth the Warriors of Flame.

"I think I hit the jackpot." I scan the spell. Besides the blood, the materials seem normal—white candles, salt.

Of the sky and of the ground,
We call the Night Warrior's spirits down.
Unto the light and unto the dark,
Mighty warriors look into our hearts.
Hear our pleas and ascend to Earth.
I give the blood of three to assist your birth.
We call the Night Warriors from their slumber.

"We're going to need an amulet that will hold up to channeling the power of the founding bloodlines."

"That's going to be one hell of an amulet. Their energies are all potent and very different."

"It's lucky I have someone who excels at making them then, isn't it?" I ask.

Aim rolls her eyes. "Suck up. I'm already thinking up a few things."

My pocket vibrates, and my mind immediately turns to Mrs. Tanaka. Fishing it out, I'm stunned to see Ari's name.

"Hello?"

"Ezra. I need you to come home."

"What?"

"Mom is acting strange."

Sighing, I peer up at the ceiling. "I don't have time for this."

"She's out all hours of the night and distant."

"Maybe she's not as unaffected by Aunt Hisa's death as she let on. We all grieve differently."

"It feels like more than that."

"You know her way better than me, Ari. What exactly do you expect me to do?"

"Come and check it out?"

"When I get the time."

"Make it sooner, rather than later."

"Fine." I hang up and shake my head.

"Everything okay?" Aim asks.

"I'm sure it is. Mom isn't fawning over him, and suddenly the world's ending. She's got her eyes set on bigger prizes now. He should get used to being placed on the back burner." My phone vibrates, and I look at the text. "We're starting to get traction for the emergency meeting. If you're okay here, I want to visit Mrs. Tanaka."

"Don't take that situation on yourself, Ez. It's not your fault."

"I'm the one who led them there."

"Whoever is doing this, knew she was a threat. She's one of the few people who could put all the puzzle pieces together, Ez. She was a target."

I grunt. We'll have to agree to disagree. Right now, it feels like everything is falling in around me, and if I could, I would've kept her out of this entirely, too.

"Let me know when you've ironed out all the kinks."

"Mmhmm."

She never looks up from the sketch pad where she's drawing and scribbling. Smirking, I stand and make my way out of her house, leaving the historical book for her to reference. Slipping the *Book of the Dead* back into the bag enchanted to be bigger on the inside, I head out.

Walking down the hall, I'm struck by the sense of vampire. Quickening my speed, I hurry toward Mrs. Tanaka's room. When I reach the doorframe, I'm surprised to see Waylon. Her bleached denims are rolled up at the ankles, and paired with a pair of white tennis shoes, and an off the shoulder black T-shirt.

"What are you doing here?" She's the last person I want to see right now.

"Same as you, checking in on her." Drawing her shoulders back, she sits up straight in the chair, and places her feet on the floor. Pressing her hands onto the tops of her thighs, she leans forward. Her curly side-ponytail bounces.

"You don't even know her," I say suspiciously.

"No, but she got hurt on our watch, helping us. It's the least I could do." She shrugs.

I want to believe this is a selfless act, but the memories of her denial are still too fresh in my mind. Would she give a stranger more consideration than she did me?

"Did Lazarus order you to be here?"

"No," she snaps. Standing from her chair, she entwines her fingers. "You can't paint me as a villain in every situation because I screwed up."

"Screwed up? You proved how untrustworthy you could be. And that was with me seeing you almost every day. Who knows what you've turned into now?"

Her shoulders stiffen, and her brown eyes lighten to glowing amber.

"Careful. You want to keep that temper in check."

"I'm not going to let you treat me like this. I deserve better."

"Not from me you don't."

I blink, and she's in front of me. "I smell your fear." Her nostrils flare. "Do you really think picking fights is going to stop what's meant to happen? We're supposed to lead everyone to victory together. How can that possibly happen when we're constantly at each other's throats?"

"This is business—"

"It could never be that black and white between us."

"You were here first, so I'll leave." I step back, and she steps forward.

"Stop running away from me."

"Oh, *you* want me to stay?" I ask sarcastically.

"I wanted you to stay then, Ezra, but not at the cost of your life."

"Such a convenient excuse." I look away, unable to peer into the glistening amber pools full of sorrow.

Her hand shoots out, and she cups my cheek. "Convenient for who? Do you think it didn't rip my heart out to abide by their rules? For the Lovecraft Clan, only the group exists. You aren't allowed any outside influences. They're self-contained, all-consuming, and controlling." She lets her hand drop and her body trembles. "They isolate you and fill your mind with their belief system, warping your sense of right and wrong until you'll do anything they want. We were never the family they promised. We were weapons and game pieces they could use for their own benefit." She balls her fists.

"What did they do to you?" I whisper, unable to remain stoic.

She blinks, and I see a universe of pain in her gaze. "They broke me, and for a while, I didn't know or care who I was. It was easier that way."

"What changed?"

"I can't tell you that," she whispers.

I sigh. "Always with the secrets." She flinches. "Or is this to keep me 'safe' again?" I use air quotes.

"This is me not ready to talk about something I'm still working through."

"Right. I'll give you the benefit of the doubt … never."

"You—" The overhead lights flicker. A wave of darkness slithers its way through the hospital. I pause. "Did you sense that?" she asks softly.

"Yeah, I did," I whisper back. The hospital is full of spirits in various stages of transition. Some are upset. Others are lost or confused. People are good and bad, with varying levels of positive and negative thoughts and emotions. Their energy reflects that after death. This is different. I walk to the door, open it, and look to the left and right. The lights are going wild all down the hallway.

In the flashes of light, I glimpse the inky blank shadows creeping over the walls and along the floor toward us from all sides.

Slamming the door, I tense as fight or flight kicks in.

She places her hand on my arm. "What did you see?"

"Shadows that move."

"We need to get out of here," she whispers.

"Except, I don't know if they're here for us or her." I nod toward the still form of Mrs. Tanaka.

"Her family has laid down powerful blood spells. They should hold. Especially if we lead them away."

"Okay." I glance around the room. "We're on the third floor."

"Vampire …"

"You can't manipulate the air."

"I can. I did a lot of learning over the past year. It was part of why I needed to be on my own. I was ignorant to so much."

"Because there were no mentors you could get? Necromancers have a school. I find it hard to believe you couldn't find something similar."

"Who would have told me about it, Ez? You have no clue how much I was on my own in my existence. I was made by a rogue, and from there, I taught myself how to survive. I didn't know the basic things. I'm different now." She rushes over to the window.

"Get ready to move fast. The moment I break this, I'm sure an alarm will sound." Reaching back, she punches through the thick glass panes like crepe paper. Yanking out the remaining pieces, she offers me her hand. "Let's go."

Backed into a corner, I push my apprehension and pride aside and take her outstretched hand. Stepping up onto the platform, I take a deep breath before we step out of the empty frame, and cast a cloaking spell. The air rushes past me, stealing my breath. Our descent slows and we settle onto the ground on the sidewalk.

"Holy shit."

She chuckles. "I know. That never gets old."

The street light above our head clicks off. The shuffle of feet in the distance are followed by an intense scent of decaying flesh and unsettling dead energy. Waving my hand, I turn on the light, and reveal pale creatures in various stages of decay. Tags flutter on their toes and stitches line their torso, indicating recent embalming.

"They animated bodies in the morgue," I whisper.

She grimaces. "If they're fresh, why are they breaking down so rapidly?"

"Dark magic takes its pound of flesh … literally. It warps, and since their souls are already departed, the only thing left to corrupt is the body."

Lifting its hand, the heavyset male ripped the stitches

from his pale blue lips. "Give us the book, and you might survive this."

I clench my jaw. *So, this is about the Book of the Dead.*

"Have you ever heard of a library?" Waylon taunts.

"I own a lot of books. You'll have to be a bit more specific."

"The *Book of the Dead.*"

"Oh. That one. Yeah, not going to happen."

"You chose this," the man warns.

"I feel the exact same way about you." Holding up my palm, I send a blast of fiery energy out to surround him. Ghouls are terrified by fire. Screaming, he backs up. The shuffle of more feet comes from the left. Turning my head, I find a small army of about fifteen approaching.

"Waylon."

She turns her head and follows my gaze. "Oh. My. God."

"Run."

Springing into action, the dark-haired woman in her mid-thirties lunges at us, making an impossible leap. Ghouls are powerful. The magic pushes them to do things a normal human can't, and they don't feel pain or remorse to slow them down. Moving in, they try to herd us, forming a semi-circle of dead flesh. Darting forward, a young male rushes me. I shove my hands out palms first, and force him back. Another creature approaches me from my blindside. A sickening crunch explodes in my ear as Waylon snaps its back in a backbreaker move that would've made the Dwayne "The Rock" Johnson proud. Seeing it try to continue after her with jerky movements is disturbing.

Reaching back, I pull the sword I strapped on and shielded beneath my coat. The sword slides free from its sheath and cuts the air like butter. The metal sings as I take my stance, and feel the energy gather. I track the ghouls with my eyes. The petite, white-haired woman with paper-thin skin, a skeletal frame, and gnarled fingers comes at me with her bony digits curved into claws. I react, slicing up her abdomen and back down. The scent of searing flesh floods my nostrils, turning my stomach. Smoke billows into my eyes as fire engulfs her from the inside out, turning her into ashes as she tries to scream against her stitched-shut mouth.

The sword has a mind of its own. I'm moving before my human brain can fully register it. Spinning, slashing, and giving chase, I cut down the bloodless fiends. Breathing heavily and sweating profusely, I stand among a pile of ash with Waylon at my back. We've dispatched of them together, watching one another's back.

"That sword is amazing AF."

I let out a hysterical laugh. "Yeah. It is." I turn my head and give her a once over. "Are you okay?"

She holds up her arm. Deep gouges heal before my eyes.

"Nothing time can't heal. You?"

"I'm okay." Removing a cloth from my bag, I wipe away the bits of flesh.

"We make a good team."

"When we're destroying things, we certainly do."

Huffing, she crosses her arms over her chest.

"I don't understand the two of you."

The familiar voice makes me jump. "You need bells attached to you," I mutter.

"Why fight the inevitable?" Prince Baylard asks, falling into step beside us as we leave the scene.

"What are you talking about?" I ask, not sure the fae even lives in the same time and place as we do.

"You're a rare example of a soul bond. Nothing you do will break it." His brow furrows. "I suppose you could ignore it or avoid one another, but no one else will ever feel as right."

"The hell are you saying?"

"I can see karmic cords. And you two are bound by the silver cord."

"I refuse to believe destiny is predetermined," Waylon says.

"Hmmm ... more like heavily suggested," Price Baylard remarks flippantly. "I see you've used my brother's sword tonight."

Still reeling from his unwarranted truth bomb, I struggle to wrap my head around his next bombshell.

"You're related to Eitri?"

He inclines his head. "I would've suspected him, but he's not ruling and just as displeased about the way things are being run as I am. Why else would he help humans?"

"Because he had a marker called in," Waylon suggests.

"Oh, it's rare that we get caught without an exit strategy."

The sly expression makes my stomach hurt. *What's he getting out of this, other than amusement? How can we trust him truly?*

"I have a score to settle, necromancer. I missed out on very important things while I was bound in that spider's web. My need for vengeance outweighs my desire for trickery at the moment."

"How can we believe you?"

"You shouldn't, yet it makes my words no less true. You and I have more in common than you know. When the time is right, I'll enlighten you." For a moment, his eyes take on a serious expression that frightens me to the core.

What could mean so much to him? What's this help going to cost me? Cost all of us?

CHAPTER TWELVE

H ave you looked outside today?"

"What?" I ask groggily as I rub my eyes to find Aim hovering over me.

"I know you're exhausted, but you have to get up now. The brown stuff has hit the fan."

Propping myself up against the headboard, I sigh. "What's happening now?"

"Can't you feel it?" She places her finger against her lips.

Closing my eyes, I shake off the final tendrils of sleep and focus on the present. Shoulders slumped, I tap into the environment. My eyes pop open.

"What the hell is going on?" The energy outside is

electric. Like a powder keg with a long fuse lit and slowly traveling toward the dynamite, ready to explode.

"All hell broke loose last night … literally. The barrier between this world and the other failed."

"Is it still down?"

"No, but that brief moment was long enough to let some particularly nasty things lose."

"The huntsmen?"

"If they came, they're hiding well. Regardless, we need to finish this amulet and call forth the Night Warriors. I spent all night working on it. The amulet represents all the elements and the twelve zodiac signs. It's made from gold, and has a bloodstone as its central jewel."

"All right, let me get in the shower."

"I'll get the coffee going."

My phone vibrates. The sight of Ari's name makes me roll my eyes. *Not now.*

Throwing back the sheets, I swing my legs over the side of the bed and force my body out of the downy heaven I'd passed out in. Shuffling like a woman three times my actual age, I make it to the shower, squinting against the bright light pouring in from the windows. I turn the water as hot as I can stand it, strip down, and step underneath the spray. Head bowed, I try to go over what I know and how I can help. We need to fix what's broken. The time for talking, negotiation, and debate is past. The world is about to crumble around our ears while we play politics. The world feels wrong. Like there are more dead than living in this place. *Right now, that might be true.*

It's the definition of hell on earth with the dead walking, outnumbering the living. *Is this how the apocalypse really starts? Not with zombies, but spirits?* If they gain enough energy to start possessing, we're in a whole other mess of trouble. Cutting the shower short, I dry off, wrap the black towel around my waist, and hurry back to my room. After dressing in my usual black jeans and T-shirt, I tame my hair with a bit of hair mousse and arm myself for survival. I wear protective amulets on my wrists and around my neck. A carefully crafted leather belt with power-boosting sigils is threaded through the belt loops of my skinny jeans.

Easing on my black combat boots, I run my thumb over the protective runes carved into the worn leather. After last night, I'm not taking any chances. Adding my Katana to the mix, I cast a quick glamour to hide the bulk and follow my nose toward the aroma of roasting coffee beans. The amulet resting on the table is a thing of beauty.

I give a low whistle. "Nice work, Aim."

"Thank you." She smiles at me over the rim of her cup of java juice.

Grabbing my travel mug, I take a drink of the scalding liquid.

"What do you want to do first?" she asks.

Climb back into the bed and sleep for another twenty-four hours.

"I'm sure I have a stack of voice mails to return. I'll call around and see what everyone's take is on the situation and what they want to do. I think it's going to take all of the necromancers and witches we can manage to do this patch job." Choking on my pride, I pull my phone from my back pocket and call Waylon.

"Hey, you heard?"

"I felt the minute I woke. What's going on with it?"

"We've been assembling groups in the house to help put out fires, and having conference calls with other clans, witches, and wolves. I'm not saying they like working with us, but the alternative isn't feasible." She sighs heavily, sounding dog-tired.

"You sound beat."

"You know the saying 'I'll sleep when I'm dead'?" Waylon asks.

"Yeah?"

"I feel cheated. 'Cause I'm dead and there's no rest to be found."

I snicker. If she can make jokes, she's okay. "Have you seen our favorite winged one?"

"Not since his abrupt departure last night."

"You're benched until sunset, so Aim and I are going

to check in with the other necromancers." Grabbing my keys off the counter, I shake them at Aim, who nods.

"Lazarus wants you to see where the necromancers stand in all this."

"As soon as I have anything to tell, I'll pass it along." The energy shifts in the room, and I find myself mere inches away from royalty once more. I stop myself from rolling my eyes. Last thing I need is a wicked curse from his royal highness.

"Fair beauty, it's been too long since these eyes have had the pleasure of seeing you once more."

I follow his admiring gaze to my best friend. She'd be a feast for a faerie's eyes with her white baby doll dress with a pink floral pattern and white kittens around the bottom hem. Her Peter Pan collar is trimmed in pink ribbon with three buttons down the front. White stockings adorn her long legs, and disappear into the pink flats that crisscross in the front. Her pink and white trench coat completes the look.

She curtseys. "Thank you, Prince."

"So formal. Call me Baylard."

The hair on the back of my neck stands on end. Things never end well between humans and faeries.

"We were just on our way out." I position my body in between them.

"I'll accompany you." He offers his arm to Aim, who looks at me, bewildered.

I give a small nod. The last thing we want to do is insult him. It takes everything in me not to snatch her away. The content expression on Baylard's face is off. It doesn't fit the personality I've become used to seeing with him. I watch them suspiciously as we travel outside. The syrupy feeling of otherworldly energy clings to me like humidity in the summer. My eyes dart back and forth, chasing the massive snowflakes coming in sideways.

"When did this roll in?" I ask.

"Sometime overnight. It's Mother Nature's response to the unnatural order being disrupted. The news is calling it a freak snowstorm."

Distracted as we enter the car, I pull off the property and realize just how much the wards had kept at bay. My jaw drops at the cloudy gray sky and nearly a foot of snow. Branches sag underneath the weight of the freshly fallen frozen precipitation. My hands clench the wheel as I roll carefully through the whiteout.

"Stop the car."

"What?" I glance back in the rearview mirror to see the fae prince tense and sit up straight.

"Stop the car. Now."

Pressing the pedal down, I pull over onto the shoulder.

"Whatever you see, don't get out of the car."

"What's going on?" Aim asks.

"This isn't natural snow. It's from my realm." Opening

the door, he steps outside, and the snow parts like the Red Sea, carving a pathway for the prince, who is now glowing like a phosphorous beacon.

"You can show yourself now. Unless you're too frightened." Baylard turns around slowly in a circle. Large icicles come in sideways, but he dodges them without breaking a sweat. "You waited too long. The lands have begun to realize I'm not dead."

"Lies. The rightful ruler is on the throne!" The ethereal voice seems to come from everywhere at once.

"We both know that's not true. Come on, Vidia. Aren't you tired of being an errand girl?"

"I will always stand for the crown."

A flurry of ice knives fly at Baylard, who moves like a tow-haired ninja. Twisting his body, he spins like a corkscrew, obscuring his frame with a whirl of snow. Ice bands shoot out, wrapping around an invisible body.

"Gotcha." Planting his feet, Baylard yanks. A woman becomes visible. Thin, blue lips pull back from a row of blinding white teeth. Her silver hair is pulled up in an intricate bun, and black leather adorns her slender frame.

"Not quite." Slashing downward with her arms, she breaks the ice rope. She kicks up powdery dust, sending a wicked icicle out from her palm. Baylard dodges it, only to be skimmed by a follow-up shot. His eyes flash white, and snow and ice attach themself to the mysterious female warrior, turning her into an ice sculpture. Tottering back and forth, the ice explodes as the woman frees herself. Tense, she appears to be shook.

"Tell Durin I'm coming back for my crown. You can be my messenger girl this time. Let's see who the people choose to side with."

"They'll never even hear your name."

"You think so?" He smiles, a knowing expression that apparently rattles the woman.

Narrowing her eyes, she places two fingers over her lips. "Sweet dreams, my Prince."

Blue dust falls from the sky onto Baylard's head, and his eyes flutter closed. Slumping to the ground, he lays still, and the woman winks out of view.

Aim fumbles with the door, and I lean across to still her actions. "Let's make sure she's gone before we head out there."

"He's going to freeze to death."

I grab her hand and squeeze. "Never forget what Baylard actually is, Aim. Little can actually kill him. From what I can figure, he was being drained by the spider woman for at least a year. Complacency when it comes to the folk is a dangerous thing."

She looks down. "You're right."

"Good. Now we can both go check on him." Giving her hand another gentle squeeze, I let go and open the driver's side door.

Stepping out into the frigid wind, we make our way toward his prone form. His lips are blue and his skin is only a few shades lighter than a smurf's.

"It looks like she cast a sleeping spell on him," I whisper as I kneel down beside him in the snow. His skin is cold to the touch, but his chest is moving up and down steadily enough. There's no rapid eye movement beneath his eyelids, but that might be normal for him.

"Let's get him in the car." I raise my hand to lift him, and she stills my gesture.

"I got him."

Her odd behavior starts an ache in my belly I don't have time to examine. She lifts him, stabilizing his body with her powers as we hurry back to the warmth of the vehicle. *Sure, Universe, add a bespelled prince into the mix. It's exactly what I need to make this day even more headache-inducing. It's a choose your own adventure gone terribly wrong.*

"We need to summon his brother." I glance in the rearview mirror at his prone frame.

"We should do it now?"

"I don't think this is a good place to stop." I gesture toward the white world outside the window with my thumb.

"And if waiting costs him his life? Who do you think the fae will blame?"

"Damn it." I slap the wheel and find a place to pull over once more.

Digging in my satchel, I locate a carton of salt and shake it. "Let's make this quick. The last thing we need is frostbite."

Scrambling out of the car, we lay a circle of salt for protection.

"Knife." She opens her palms.

"I can make the offering."

"No, you have your mission. This is my risk to take."

Handing her a small dagger, I grimace as she pricks her thumb and let's a few drops of the crimson red liquid fall onto the white snow. "I call you, Eitri, brother of Prince Baylard, to this time and place. Hear my request."

The gray sky darkens to a murky near black and the snow comes down harder. We step closer together to share body heat. A whistling noise precedes a wind tunnel that batters at the circle of salt. Wrapping my arm around her waist, I keep her smaller frame anchored to me as I brace against the elements. A bright light flashes. Blinking, my vision slowly adjusts to the dark-haired, angelic creature hovering above us.

"You," he whispers.

I'm not sure who he's talking to, but I'm too afraid to ask.

"Why have you called me?"

"Your brother had a run-in with Vidia. He fell unconscious."

"They've made their move," Eitri whispers more to himself than us. Gliding toward the car, he opens the door and clucks his tongue. "The dreaming curse. You'll have to be more cunning than that. I owe you a boon." He lifts his brother in his arms. "You'll see me again."

Gone in the next instant, we're left with a serious case of the shivers and more questions than answers. The high-pitched whine of a motorized vehicle has me on my feet. There's no way you could ride a motorcycle in this. We backtrack to the car. A rider appears clad in all black with a blacked-out helmet. They rest a foot onto the ground, and are flanked by two more identically clad, larger, and bulkier people.

The lid is lifted to reveal Waylon.

"What are you doing?"

"When it's this overcast," she nods her head upward, "I can do some sun."

"Is that why you smell like the devil's sunscreen?" Aim taunts.

"Yeah, we use a special blend to help, too. It's called hedging your bets." Her eyes flash amber.

"Why did you come out here like this?"

"Mrs. Tanaka is awake, and she's asking for you."

"Is she okay?"

She averts her gaze. "I think it'd be easier to show you."

I glance from Aim to Waylon, unsure of my next move.

"Go see her. I'll hold down the fort and talk with our people. I can probably get more out of them anyway," Aim remarks.

"Braggart." I toss her the keys, knowing I'm out of options. "Keep me posted on any changes."

"Likewise." Our gazes meet, and she silently threatens me in a way only your closest friend can.

I give a nod of acknowledgment. The shields on the other riders rise, and I find myself looking at a leggy, red-haired woman—Illyiah, a witch—and her tow-haired, brown-eyed, slender vampire companion, Alex. I recognize them both from the Coalition. "After the last time we went to the hospital, they're our back up."

"Moving up in the world, I see."

"Good. Hope on," Waylon says, ignoring me.

"I'm going to regret this already," I mutter as I climb onto the back and wrap my arms around her waist. Once Aim is safely locked inside of the car, she peels off, and I tighten my grip, fearing for my life.

"Don't worry. With my new senses, I'm the safest driver around," she yells over the roar of the wind and the whining engine. My hair blows back from my face, and the cold does battle with the warming spells woven into my coat.

Outside of the hospital room, two sunglass-wearing older Asian gentlemen stand guard. The family's called in reinforcements. Bowing respectfully, I wait to see if they'll let me pass. A few moments later, they give the nod, and wave us inside. The taller, bulkier, bald-headed male holds out his hand, palm up to bar Illythia and Alex. "Not them."

"It's okay. You can help protect her from out here. That's what you two were brought here anyway," Waylon says before closing the door behind her.

Stepping inside, I'm pleasantly surprised to see Mrs. Tanaka propped up in bed with pillows. Her daughter is in a chair watching the television.

"Mrs. Tanaka, I can't tell you how happy I am to see you awake."

Her thin lips curve up into a smile. "It takes more than that to end an old woman like me.

"Come, sit. You and Waylon." She pats the bed on the opposite side of her daughter.

I pause. There's something not quite right about her gestures. *She's just had a serious brain trauma, what do you expect, Ezra?* Sinking down onto the bed, I take her offered hand.

"During my time away, I saw a great many things.

Wondrous, horrible things." She gulps. "Things I can't fully remember, and others, I wish I could forget. A change is coming, and before it can take place, old systems have to break so new ones can rise from their ashes. There's gonna be pain, but from that, there will be hope." She pats my hand. "My vision was taken, but I see from a new perspective now."

"Mrs. Tanaka? You're blind?"

"And yet now I see," she adds.

"I'm so sorry." I drop my head.

"There's no need for guilt. I don't blame you for things far beyond your control. But I come bearing a message. Your family is in grave danger, and if you want even a fraction to survive, you're going to have to fight."

My thoughts go to my brother. "Ari," I whisper.

She tilts her head to the side. "Things aren't always what they seem, Ezra."

Aunt Hisa's dream warning comes to mind. *Mom's acting weird. She's gone all hours of the night.* My chest aches. I fumble with my phone and call my brother. His phone rings, and rings, and rings … eventually going to voice mail.

A sinking sensation explodes in my belly. I have to return to the one place I hate most, the home where I grew up.

CHAPTER THIRTEEN

The two-story white home with its white railing and upper balcony stands out like an icy fortress amidst the snow still accumulating on the ground. My brother's sports car is in the driveway, along with my mother's foreign luxury SUV, but the lights are all off. Hoping off the back of the bike, I run down the walkway and up the stairs. A fowl stench creeps out from beneath the heavy doorframe. Fumbling with a set of keys I haven't used in years, I slip the key in the lock and turn the tumbler. It gives with a creak, and I push the door open.

A cloud of white vapor escapes as I step inside the home. If it's possible, it might be colder inside than it was out in the snow. Waylon tries to step inside after me and hisses. Her skin reddens, and she falls to her knees.

"Stop." I hold out my hand. "I need to do this alone."

"No."

"I can't be sure what wards or spells she's placed on the house. I won't be responsible for another person being hurt today." I wave my hand and slam the door, locking it.

"Ari," I call out, rushing through the floors as I follow his fading life force. Hitting the stairs that lead upstairs to the rooms, my hand sticks to the railing. I tear it free and peer down. My heart lurches and flies up into my throat. The thick, white coating is webbing.

"Ari." As much as I hate the pissant at times, he's my brother. I don't want anything bad to happen to him. Okay, anything deadly. Careful to keep my arms at my side, I increase my jog to a full-out run. Hitting the top of the stairway, I take a left, and make a beeline for the third door on the right. Kicking it open, I struggle to digest exactly what I'm seeing. Trussed up like a living sacrifice, Ari is pinned to the wall, arms out, eyes wide with terror. His pupils are so small; it's hard to see beyond the white.

Red hot rage explodes inside of me like lava.

"Don't take him down unless you plan to take his place."

I spin and find the woman formerly known as my

mother in the doorway in a black gown that grazes the floor. Her hair has turned snow white, and her fingernails have grown into miniature daggers. Her eyes are cold and dark, and her lips appear bloodless.

"You?"

"We both know your brother is weak. It's you who's inherited the lion's share of the power."

Her eyes flicker with excitement, and I know she wants to have me up there beside him. "How could you do this to your own son? He worshipped the ground you walked on."

"There's not going to be a place for him in the new world that's coming."

Keep her talking. This runs deeper than one woman's desire to gain power.

"What world?"

"You think the huntsmen coming back is a coincidence?" She laughs. "Silly, naïve boy. It took a lot of time, planning, and waiting for the perfect time. I won't let you undo all of that." Her voice lowers an octave. "Those not born with power must take it by any means necessary. Little by little, I seeped out energy, gathering it like interest in a bank account waiting to be cashed out."

How many people has she killed?

"You're the final piece. My wayward son come home just in time to see me ascend the throne."

"Why?"

"Hisa was old and fading. Why would I want her powers when I could have yours all shiny and new?"

"You killed her?" My hands ball into fists.

"I helped her—"

Binding her mouth shut with a spell, I throw her down the hallway and dart out of the room, mind racing. She reappears in front of me and laughs. The throaty sound sends ice into my stomach.

"Did you really think it'd be that easy?"

"How could the family line choose you?" I sneer, disgusted by the lies.

"Make it easy on me for once in your life. Stop running."

"Never going to happen."

She smirks. "Always the hard way." A swirling black and purple ball of energy gathered in her open palms. The darkness spoke to her evil intentions. Magic was neutral intention, and users made it shades of black and white. Most people say you fight fire with water. I prefer to do it with more fire. I'm one with the darkness moving between the two worlds. Reaching into the earth, the land beyond existence, I channel it through my body. For my aunt, for my brother, and the nameless others, I unlock the door inside of me that I've guarded for years.

Unbound, the door flies open, and a stream of energy

bursts forth, wrapping around her like a see-through ribbon. Her arms are pressed into her sides, and she squirms.
It's a poetic justice.

"This won't hold me forever." The words are screamed
inside of my mind.

"No, just long enough," I summon my brother from
his room upstairs, "to do this." Snagging the keys off the
hook by the door, I make my way outside.

"What the hell were you thinking?" Waylon explodes.

"That family drama should stay between family. It's
her, Waylon."

Waylon furrows her brow. "Who? What are you
talking about?"

"The sorceress. It's been my mother all along." The
words form a lump in my throat. Knowing I come from
someone so evil makes me sick. "We need to go. What
I've done won't hold her long. Not when she's juiced up
from all the power she's high-jacked."

"A new world is coming and I'll be queen." Mother's
words play in my head as we quickly evacuate the area.
"Whatever called the Hunt back, she was in on it. She
said as much." I shake my head. How could she be so
selfish and short-sighted?

The snowdrift to the left explodes. Heavy chunks of
ice slam down onto the roof and pelt the windows like
rocks.

"Floor it," Waylon yells.

Increasing my speed, I dodge the flying icebergs. A medium-sized ice boulder clips the right side of the car and we spin out. Fingers clamped on the wheel, I use my entire body to keep us from going off road. The car comes to a complete stop in the middle of the street. Breathing hard, I remove my trembling hands from the wheel and place them in my lap. My mother appears in the middle of the road with a white horn in her hand. Placing it to her lips, she blows. The loud blast shakes the road beneath the car, knocks the snow off the trees, and rips the veil between this world and the next down.

The Night Hunt has officially begun. The bottom drops out of my stomach.

"We're not ready." Waylon's voice trembles.

Punching the gas, I floor it. We swerve to the left and right, but I never slow down intentionally. Hell has broken loose and we're sitting ducks. Hoofs sound in the distance. Red eyes glow from the forest that seems to be closing in around us. Pulling up Bluetooth audio, I call Aim.

"Aim?"

"Did you hear the horn?"

"My mother's the one who blew the damn thing," I bark.

"Jesus."

"He wasn't a part of it, trust me. What's happening over there?"

"I've gathered the blood of the families that first created the night warriors and called them."

"Where should we meet?" I ask. The phone grows statically. "Aim? Aim!"

"Laz … Lazar … s."

"Lazarus'?" I ask.

The blue tooth has disconnected. Glancing down I realize my phone is dead.

"I think that's all we're going to get," Waylon whispers.

The trunk crumples under a heavyweight, and the front tires lift off the ground.

"Get out of the car," I yell. Yanking open the doors with my powers I tumble into the snow, roll onto all fours, and scramble to get purchase on the slushy mess, so I can get Ari out of the back. Hefting him across my shoulders, I gain my feet and do my best imitation of a run. In six inches of snow, it's more wading than running as my feet sink down over and over again. An eerie howl pierces the recently fallen night. The moon is a fat red circle hanging low against the blue-black sky. Waylon appears beside me. Biting her wrists, she holds it toward me.

"No."

"If you could hear how close they are, and how hard your heart is working while you carry Ari, you'd already be chugging right now." She shoves her wrist underneath my nose.

I allow her to bring it to my mouth. The salty, metallic liquid floods my mouth. Sucking at the pinprick wounds, I let the hot liquid flow down my throat, knowing I'm crossing a line I can't return from. I can feel the blood bolstering my strength and lending me its supernatural bonuses. She pulls away, and I lick the residue off my lips.

"Better?"

"Better," I agree.

She takes off like a jackrabbit, and I follow. The trees blur as I push my body to its top speed. Despite the speed, the hounds and the horses seem to gain. I trust her sense of direction as we weave through the forested areas. A translucent spirit rushes past us. Then another, and another.

"They keep the souls they capture," Waylon whispers.

The thought is more horrifying than death itself. Being stuck in a murderous loop. Wood splinters next to my head. The quiver of the arrow wiggles.

Grabbing her hand, I cast a cloaking spell, and we give chase.

"We can smell your rotten stench, witch. No spell will hide you."

Ignoring the low-pitched voice, we run once more. My foot catches a thick root, and we tumble to the ground.

A horse neighs too close for comfort. Using my powers, I break a branch on the opposite side of the woods, rustling brush. The black horse jumps into view, and the skeletal hunter is highlighted by the moonlight. He looks starved and crazed. Cheekbones protrude, and eyes are sunken into the gaunt face. Wild scarlet eyes rimmed with dark rings are revealed in the open head armor.

Blocking our scent, I remain totally still. She buries her face in my chest, and we wait. The huntsman gives chase, following the fake trail. We wait a few moments before continuing on our way.

"Ezra," she cries out seconds before a rope tightens around her waist. Her fingers are ripped from mine, and she's pulled away into the darkness.

"No." The guttural cry bursts free and I give chase without a thought for anything or anyone else. They can't have her. Resting my brother on the ground against a tree, I cast a notice-me-not spell, and give chase. Catching up to the kidnapper, I'm shocked by the dark blue form of the dark goblin. His long, hooked nose, triangular ears, and twitching tail drive home his otherness. Drool runs from the corner of his thin-lipped, cruel mouth.

"His Highness will be so pleased with me," he says gleefully.

"Not quite." I sew his mouth shut with a thought and pull out my sword. A few slashes later, he's lying on the ground, twitching as his dark blood seeps onto the forest floor. Unbinding Waylon's waist, I offer her hand.

"You came for me."

"Yes." I'd always come for her. Denying it wouldn't change the truth.

"I don't think that was part of the Hunt."

"His Highness," I repeat the words. "He said his highness."

"Well, we knew someone had to re-work the contracts."

"How far away from the Coalition's home are we?" I ask.

"Fifteen miles."

We return to Ari, and I take a deep breath. "Picture the Coalition living room in your mind." The blood flowing between us strengthens our bonds. I slip inside of her mind like an expert thief, extracting the imagery. Gathering my strength, I hold my breath and send out a rush of power to teleport us. We land on the floor marble floor with a sickening crunch.

"Your landings suck."

I groan as I roll onto my side. "I don't travel this way often. Be happy we didn't lose a limb or something."

"Thank God, you're here." Aim hurries over and offers her hand, pulling me to my feet as Frida does the same for Waylon. "You need to do the summoning now." She presses the gold amulet into my hand.

Rubbing a hand over my face, I nod. My energy is flagging and what I'm about to attempt is dangerous on a good day.

"I need a space—"

"It's already set up." Lazarus steps from a small room. "It's been cleansed by our witches and stocked with whatever ingredients you might need."

I pick up on the underlying message. I need to do this now.

"Help him?" I nod to my brother.

"Of course." His words are clipped. The protection on the land will only hold for so long. I enter the room, close the door behind me, and open my satchel. Drawing a circle with chalk, I follow it with salt, and settle in the center. Removing the Book of the Dead, I jerk as a surge of energy flows through me. The lights flicker, and the temperature drops. *We're too late.*

The black fog begins to fill the room, creeping in around me. Sand starts to swirl around, forming a pillar that becomes the Jackal-headed form of Anubis. I kneel immediately.

"You no longer need these parlor tricks to summon the dead, necromancer. You bring your petitions directly to me." He thumps his chest. "Ask, and I shall grant or deny, son of Anubis."

"If it pleases you, I'd like to bring back the Night Warriors."

Tapping the end of his staff against the marble floor, he clears a path in the dark smoke. Floating scales appear. They balanced back and forth before settling, and he nods.

"Rise. What you ask shall be granted."

I stand on trembling limbs. You don't get used to being in the presence of Anubis. A portal of light opens and four figures float through it. The floor becomes solid, the black fog retreats, and a large, golden door covered with hieroglyphics appears. It swings up to reveal darkness unlike any I've ever seen before. "Until we meet once more," Anubis says as he walks through the opening.

Returning my attention to the four warriors, I find myself in awe. Where the huntsmen are darkness, they're light. Their eyes glow with a righteous blue flame. They appear to be from different eras. One Caucasian male is clothed in a knight's armor with a white tunic over it. Tall and broad, with his claymore in his hand, he strikes a formidable pose.

The red-haired man beside him is dressed in a Scot's kilt and stole with a long sword and murder in his eyes. A jagged scar travels from his right temple down his cheek. The women are medium height, and sinewy. They're clad in leather armor over tunic-style dresses. One is fair-haired, and the other is dark-haired with light brown skin. Their hair is braided and pulled back from their faces. The Viking warrior women have shields, swords, and daggers attached to their sides with leather belts.

"Why do you wake us from our much-deserved rest, necromancer?" the dark-haired woman asks.

"The huntsmen are on their final ride, and thanks to outside interference, they're not playing by the rules."

"They never do, lad," the Scotsman says with a thick brogue.

"I can feel them closing in around us," the fair-haired Viking Maiden states.

"Why haven't the precautions we left held?"

I consider my words carefully. "A lot of the truth's been lost to history. The communication is poor, and while there are groups working toward it ..."

"It's not enough to undo the damage done," the Scotsman continues for me.

I nod my head, ashamed of the way we threw their gifts away.

"We come with a fee," the knight says.

I lift the amulet up.

"Do they understand what it means?" the dark-haired woman asks. "That this is a promise of unity and cooperation?"

"I'll make sure they do," I promise.

"They're bound by blood. They won't have a choice," the knight adds.

"Maybe make 'em suffer for a bite before you reveal that, huh?" the Scotsman says with a smirk.

"One more ride before we return to Valhalla?" the fair-haired warrior asks.

The Scotsman nods his head. "Aye."

"I'm always up for a bit of sword play," the dark-haired Viking says cheekily.

"Like I'm going to let all of you have the fun and glory," the knight grumbles.

The moment he stops talking, a strange blue light surrounds them, growing brighter and brighter. I raise my arm to shield my eyes from its intensity. The ozone layer hums, and my body tingles in response to the burst of power raised. A loud clap of thunder sounds and the walls shake. The door bursts open behind me and the skylight overhead shatters. Howling winds pours in, bringing snow and spirits with it.

Waylon runs to me with the others trailing behind her. She grabs my face between her hands. "Are you okay?"

I cover her hands, never taking my eyes off the scene. "I'm fine." Forming a sort of lasso, I wrap the ghosts with my powers and pull them toward me, sending them back to the other realm where they belong. As they were flashed off this plane, another batch took their place. Sweat rolled down my face and into my eyes. I ignore the burn as the witches jump in to assist. Panting, I feel them moments before they come through the gaping hole in the ceiling and the wards.

"Run."

The huntsmen pour in like grim reapers with red eyes burning and weapons high. The Night Warriors step up and engage them without hesitation. Metal clashes with metal. Sparks fly. Red and Blue light up the space like the Fourth of July firework display. Grabbing Waylon's hand, I scan the space for Aim. I spot her outside of the room, and tug Waylon behind me as I head for the door, desperate to put more space between us and them.

The huntsmen always come with a party. We need to get to the high ground to fight them. It's a struggle to make our way through the chaos with everyone moving toward the exit like salmon swimming upstream. An icy hand wraps around my shoulder.

I turn to look. Pain explodes in my face. I fly back, disoriented, with my face aflame.

"No," I hear Waylon cry out and growl.

Blinking, I focus on the small figure shooting beams of power at Waylon, who darts back and forth. *Mother.* I wipe away the blood trickling from my nose, and gain my feet.

Whoosh. I'm forced away from the two women by a rider. The horse's front feet are inches from my face as he rears back. Jumping to the left, I avoid being stomped to death. Dancing back, his eyes momentarily glue me to the spot. His jaw unhinges and a flame flies out. The heat sears my skin. Calling down water, I douse the fire. Smoke rolls from his nostrils and he snarls like a wild beast. Thin lips pull back to reveal jagged, black rooted stumps. The putrid smell of decay chokes me. I gag, and he points his broadsword at me, silently promising pain and destruction. Reaching behind me, I pull my katana from its sheath. I walk back a few steps and wait.

He swings his sword downward, and I swipe up, praying I haven't overplayed my hand, and my katana can stand up to his dark blade. Metal grinds against metal. Sparks fly. I counter his blows with my own. He brings his sword down hard, and the power forces me to my knees. Struggling to maintain my grip on my weapon, we're locked in a stalemate position.

A sharp pain explodes in my shoulder, followed by a cold burn that chills my insides. Dropping my arms, I roll away. Glancing to my left, I spy my attacker. A lesser huntsman, more decrepit and inhuman than those on horseback. Pressing my hand to the wound, I'm shocked to find it cold to the touch. The lesser rider moves in, and the mounted huntsman follows his lead. Boxed in, my gaze darts from one to the other.

They lunge as one, and I let my muscle memory take control, blocking their attacks with the moves pounded into me from a young age. Seeing a break in their on-slaught of strikes, I strike the horse. Whinnying, it rises up, kicking its hooves. Black blood oozes from the wound. Taking advantage of the distraction, I plunge the katana into the lesser huntsman's chest, twist, and pull upward. His red eyes flicker, before they dim. His body trembles, and a black cloud bursts free from the killing wound. A shrill scream fills the air.

Tightening his hold on the reins, the other huntsman charges forward. I jump to the left. *Horse versus human, I'll lose every time.* My shoulder protests as I slam into the ground, and I lose my breath.

"Well, hello, stranger."

I glance up at the wild vision of Aim grinning manically. Her pink dress is splattered with black blood and bits of things I don't want to examine too closely. She clucks her tongue. "Already hurt? I can't leave you alone for a minute, can I?" Her expression turns serious. "You okay?"

"I'll live. Are you whole?"

"I still got all my fingers." She delivers a powerful blast of energy on a lesser rushing her. Her lips part as she gasps.

"Aim." I scramble to my feet, swaying. A sword protrudes from her chest, and blood runs from the corners of her mouth.

"No," I scream, catching her as she tumbles forward. Blood races in my ears. I hold her close as my vision blurs. I glance up and scream, unleashing my rage in a steady stream of energy that consumes the two skeletal warriors closest to me. Collapsing, I place her in my lap, and surround us with a protective barrier as I assess the damage.

"This is unacceptable." Baylard appears beside us. "You are going to be fine, my love. I vow it. I'm sorry it took me so long to return to you."

Despite her labored breathing, she lifts her lids to reveal unfocused eyes. I watch in horrified fascination as Baylard's features shift. His hair darkens, along with his eyes and voice.

"Ephraim," she whispers. Her lips curve up at the corners.

"What you must have thought of me when I failed to return."

"I always knew you—" She coughs. Her entire body shakes, and I cringe. "... would never just leave me."

"Shh. Let me heal you now." He looks at me expectantly, and I allow him to enter the protective circle draining a large chunk of my reserves. I watch in awe as the flesh repairs. He gently takes her fragile form into his own lap, and I drop my arms. He can protect her in ways I never could, and the battle has yet to be won.

Numb, I stand to view the carnage. Bodies lay strew

about on the floor along with small piles of ashes and bone. Blood, black and red is everywhere. In the corner, the Scotsman and the knight have a horseback huntsman cornered. Black shadows spill out of his injured form. A wail echoes through the room, blowing the widows. His armor falls to the floor with a loud clank, and some of the lesser huntsmen fade. Others age. What's left of their flesh melts away to reveal bone, and their movements slow.

"The riders are the key to ending this," the fair-haired shield maiden yells. "Everyone with me." She lifts her shield and gives a wild cry that spurs the rest of us.

Rushing forward with her, I clear the path for the Night Warriors, flinging spells, cutting down skeletal huntsmen with my katana, and using brute force, as I kick, punch, and claw. Miniature bombs continue to detonate as the evil is dismantled one rider at a time. A large flash goes off in front of me, and I'm knocked sideways. My ears ring. Blinking, I try to focus as my vision swims. I stumble like a drunk as I turn to locate my attacker.

My mother's face appears in front of me.

"This family is mine to rule." Her icy breath sobers me.

"What did you do to Waylon?"

"That thing turned you against your family and still you seek her out?"

Panic begins to sink in as I scan the insanity, and can't find Waylon. "No, you did that all on your own."

She redirects her attention to me, and her hands crackle with purple and black energy.

Despite my feelings toward her, I'm not prepared to battle the woman who gave me life. Locking my emotions down inside, I stand to my full height. "I asked you a question, Mother."

"She's where she belongs. Don't worry, she's going to enjoy her first sunset soon."

My stomach bottoms out. "Tell me where she is."

"Yield to me."

"I don't believe I will."

"Then, you'll both die." She lands a ball of energy to my gut, doubling me over. A one-two combination lifts me off my feet. Slammed into the wall, I slide down on the floor. Pushing up onto my knees, I throw up a mirror shield. Her bolt of energy returns to her, throwing her off her feet. She cackles. "Still unwilling to fight for what matters?" She lands on her feet. "How long do you think these avoidance tactics will hold out?" Snapping her fingers, she surrounds me in a ring of fire. The flames jump high as they move in like I'm doused with gasoline.

Extinguishing them with water, I bind her. Arms glued to her sides she wiggles to free herself.

"Where. Is. She?" I ask slowly.

"Where I should've put her years ago." She breaks the bind, and we both cast a spell. Our magic clashes. Magenta against purple. She forces me back, and I regain the lost territory.

"Yield." She grits her teeth and pushes forward.

Bracing my feet, I hold my ground. I shake my hands, concentrating on her mind, returning all the pain she's inflicted. Screaming, she grabs her head. *"She can't take the power."* The voice in my head sounds suspiciously like Hisa. *"You are the rightful leader of the Zaan family. Do not ask, command."*

"Tell me where Waylon is."

Her eyes bulge, and her head twitches.

"Now."

Her mouth opens against her will. "On the roof of your home."

"Your cruelty knows no boundaries. I banish you, Kiku Zaan. From this day forth—"

"No!" she screams.

"Silence."

Her lips clamp together.

"You shall no longer be recognized as an acting member of the Zaan family." I take away the things that matter most to her—power and prestige.

"Bring Waylon back."

Her head twists to the right. She grits her teeth as she resists the command.

"Now."

She screams, bending over as her stubborn pride wins out over the pain she's inflicting onto herself. There's a sickness inside of her I don't understand. Clutching her upper thighs, she slowly sinks to the floor. She bows her head, and Waylon appears in front of me, panting.

"What?"

I cup her face. "You're safe. She will never lay a hand on you again."

She throws her arms around my neck, and I allow myself to enjoy the embrace.

A roar of victory goes up. The air lightens, and the veil begins to mend as things are reset. A portal opens. The swirling darkness takes back the creatures it delivered at our doorsteps. Screams of terror and pain rise up in a chorus of anguish. Bleeding, broken, and weak, we watch as the dawn of a new day is born in the ashes and ruin of the present.

"Ezra." My mom reaches out for me as she begins to glide across the floor toward the same portal. "No, we had a deal!" she screams. "Durin." A low growl was torn from the earth. Crackling a slit appeared in the air, and a swirling mass of silver began to work in opposition to the one claiming what was left of the huntsmen.

"A far portal," I whisper.

Mother launches her body toward the new escape and

I spring forward. A hand on my shoulder, stops my progress. I try to shrug the small hand off, and find myself rooted to the spot. Turning to peer over my shoulder, I see Oba, whole and glowing.

"You're not ready for the fight you'd find waiting on the other side of that portal." Her gaze moves over to the area where Aim and Baylard. Ephraim. Whatever he wants to be called stand "There are things that must take places first. Learn to lead the Zaan family and remain vigilant." The portal seals itself and I know I've lost my chance.

Raising up on her tiptoes, she kisses my forehead, and I close my eyes, soaking up her love. "I will always be here when you need me most. You take good care of him, Way."

"If he'll let me," she whispers, peering up at me hopefully through her thick lashes.

"I think you've both learned how important it is to hold on to what's precious." She smiles before moving away.

There are so many unanswered questions. *Did she kill her own sister? How many victims were there over the years?* But in the end, those things won't change the past. I glance down at the woman in my arms. Right now, I have a future to figure out. My mother and I will meet again on the field of battle. And I'll be ready.

"We've earned our rest, necromancer. We want to go back to sleep," the Scotsman says.

"But first, we'll be doing this differently. Left up to your own devices, you forget so quickly that you're better together," the dark-haired Viking warrior interjects. "The one that holds the key to our summons and the woman connected to him."

"What?" I ask in unison with Waylon.

"You two are in charge of forming and running a council to keep the veil strong and the events of this night alive. Then the past becomes legend, and then nothing more than a distant memory, and history repeats. Perhaps next time, we won't be so lucky."

"But the huntsmen are gone, right?" Waylon asks.

"Aye, lass. But there's always another evil waiting in the wings."

I open my mouth to protest, but the knight's narrowed gaze makes me think better of it.

"Thank you for your help. You've earned the rest I owe you." Releasing Waylon, I ignore the eyes fixed on us and guide them back to the room where I call Anubis' golden gate and watch as they travel back to where they came from.

Life has a sick sense of humor. I've become the king of

a kingdom I never truly wanted. I'm bound to the woman who once shattered my heart, but saved my life, and proved love was an action verb. There's no defining what we have, but it's something, and that's a start.

Trying my hand at an honest to God friendship with my brother for the first time in my life has been an experience. Especially with him living with me in Aunt Hisa's old house. I can't blame the guy for not wanting to go back home after everything that happened. I've relocated back to Snoqualmie, but I still take my Seattle jobs. It helps me keep my head on straight, and gives me a valid reason to escape the politics I've been sucked into. I can't say what the future holds for certain, but my plate's a lot fuller than it once was.

The Story continues in May 2020 with Baylard& Aim in

ROYAL BATTLE

Only one can wear the crown.

About the Author

Isa Mikaelson is a USA Today Bestselling author starting a new Penname for YA. She lives in Cincinnati with her two daughters and husband. She is known for her strong female leads, detailed fantastical worlds, and compelling romance infused plots. Her mind is a treasure trove of paranormal, historical, and various other random facts.

You can follow her here:

INSTAGRAM
@isa.mikaelson

FACEBOOK
www.facebook.com/Isa-Mikaelson-100512598193877